DEARLY DEPARTED

A 1960s Cozy Mystery

CARLY WINTER

Edited by
DIVAS AT WORK EDITING

Cover Design
MARIAH SINCLAIR: THECOVERVAULT.COM

Westward Publishing / Carly Fall, LLC

This book is for my mother. As a young woman in the 1960s, she longed to become a stew to see the world. Her family forbade it.

So, here you go mom.

Love you.

The year is 1965 and Patty Byrne is flying high as stewardess... until her life crashes when she finds her neighbor murdered.

While cooperating with the police, she meets FBI agent Bill Hart, who shows an interest in both her and the victim's activities. When he asks Patty to introduce him to a couple of the suspects she knows, she immediately agrees, harboring groovy visions of leaving her stewardess job behind and becoming the first female FBI agent.

But as they dive deeper into the case, it only becomes more confusing. When Patty's life is threatened, she realizes murder investigations aren't for the faint of heart. Can she untangle the web of clues to find the killer, or will she be the next victim?

Chapter 1

PUSHING MY WAY THROUGH AN ANTI-WAR PROTEST IN the streets of San Francisco carrying a suitcase was not my idea of a good time. All around me people yelled, *One, two, three four! We don't want your stupid war!* as they marched down the street, their fists in the air. However, there were hundreds of them, and somewhere in the crowd up ahead there seemed to be a traffic jam. I was caught in a sea of angry demonstrators.

"Excuse me," I said as I became jostled between two men. "Just trying to get through, please."

They ignored me. For people who said they only wanted world peace, they sure were low on manners. Forced to become more aggressive, I gave one of them an elbow to the ribs, and he finally stepped aside and allowed me to pass.

My cab had dropped me off a block away from my building due to the protests jamming the streets. I had the option to either attempt to move through them to get to my apartment or wait them out. Considering I'd just gotten off work, I really needed to get home to replenish my supplies and do a load of laundry before returning to the airport first thing in the morning for another flight. A bubble bath and a glass of wine wouldn't be a bad idea, either.

"Excuse me," I yelled again, trying to maneuver my way through. "I need to get home!"

The woman glanced over at me, then nudged her companion. They had a few brief words, and the hulking man standing over six feet muscled his way over to me. His long brown hair hung down the sides of his face, John Lennon style.

"You a stewardess?" he asked as he studied my uniform, a navy-blue pencil skirt, matching blazer, white blouse and a red and blue scarf.

"Yes. I have to get home! It's just down the block a bit!" Someone knocked into me from behind and I teetered on my heels and almost kissed the pavement until the John Lennon wannabe grabbed my elbow and set me upright.

He took my suitcase and kept his grip on my arm, then pushed through the crowd with me in tow. When we broke through the swarm of people and he deposited me on the sidewalk, I sighed in relief. "Thank you so much," I said, taking my suitcase from him. "I really appreciate your help."

"Sure. Things can get pretty riled up during the demonstrations."

I nodded and tucked a lock of black hair behind my ear just as someone shoved me from behind once again. "They certainly can," I muttered as I caught my balance.

"Are you for the war?" he asked and I answered with a grin. I had a strict policy in place not to discuss politics or religion with anyone, especially strangers.

Just as I was about to thank him again and give him a non-answer, a group of people came around the block, marching right toward the anti-war demonstrators.

Right on!

Take Saigon!

Victory to the Vietcong!

Uh-oh. A clash of pro and anti-war protestors that would most likely dissolve into violence. It had been happening all over the country.

"I better get inside," I said as the huge man turned to his enemy, raised his hand in the air and began yelling.

I hustled into my apartment building and almost choked on the smoke in the lobby. A metal garbage can had been set ablaze and our super stood over it with a fire extinguisher.

"Mr. Killian!" I shouted as I covered my nose and mouth with my hand and started to cough. "What in the world happened?"

"The anti-war protestors came in here and lit it on fire," he said, spraying the can once again.

"Oh, my goodness!"

"Dang kids don't know what the heck they're talking about with all their chants and destruction," he growled with his cigarette hanging out the side of his mouth. After setting down the fire extinguisher, he strode over to the door and glanced out, muttering under his breath. "You better get yourself upstairs, little lady," he said, turning to me. "Things are getting a bit wild outside and may spill indoors again. Get yourself to safety."

I nodded and headed for the stairs, not bothering to take the elevator. The crackling of fear up my spine drove me to hustle as fast as my tired feet could carry me. If Mr. Killian thought I could be in danger, I wanted to remove myself from the area as quickly as possible.

On the third floor, I fished my keys from my purse as I kicked off my shoes and picked them up. Once inside my apartment, I locked the door and sighed in relief, until I noted the mess.

The smell of cigarettes still hung in the air, beer bottles littered the coffee table, and dirty plates sat in the sink. Nylons and bras had been laid over the lampshades and the back of chairs to dry. I shared the one-bedroom apartment with another stew named Donna. I loved her like a sister, but she definitely had a problem with her drinking and partying. Thankfully, our schedules rarely overlapped, but I oftentimes came home to evidence of her chaotic life.

After dropping my suitcase, I went to the window and opened it, hoping for some fresh breeze to air out the place. Unfortunately, I also had a birds-eye view of the demonstrations. The two groups yelled and screamed at each other, and after a moment, the fists flew and the blood flowed from a few noses. Sirens howled in the distance, and I suspected Mr. Killian to have called them. I cringed at the hand-to-hand fighting and quickly shut the window once again. It only drowned out a bit of the noise, so I walked over to the record player and dropped The Beatles on the turntable, set the arm to the beginning of the album and turned it up.

As I surveyed the apartment, I decided the first thing I needed to do was get out of the uniform and girdle. I dug through my drawers and located my gray sweats and red sweatshirt then disrobed, tossing the girdle on the bed. I hated the wretched thing. Since I really watched my weight, I shouldn't have to wear one, but the airline mandated it on all stews. We represented them, and flat tummies and slim hips were an absolute must in order to keep working.

On the bathroom mirror, I found a scrawled note from Donna.

Ringo is next door with Charles. Sorry about the mess. I overslept. Hope to see you soon. Love, D.

Ringo was our cat. Before retrieving him from our neighbor, I decided to clean up a bit first so I could give all my attention to the tabby. Besides, he also liked to knock over bottles and chew on cigarette butts. Having him partake in making the mess worse would only anger me.

As The Beatles crooned, I sang along as I dumped the empties into a garbage bag and dusted the tables. I soaked the dishes as I unpacked, then laid my own bras and nylons into a tub of soapy water. After picking up all of Donna's undergarments, I folded them and set them in her drawer. Every now and then I'd glance at the surreal site outside. The police had finally arrived but seemed to be having trouble breaking up the melee. Personally, I hated the very idea of war, yet, I understood sometimes it was necessary. I didn't know if the Vietnam conflict would fall under that category, but I certainly didn't like the way the veterans who came home were treated by the anti-war protestors. Yes, one had rescued me from a pickle today, but spitting on someone who has served his country did not sit well with me.

I quickly scrubbed the dishes and set them to dry next to the sink. After rinsing my clothing, I hung them up around the apartment, just as Donna had done. I couldn't wait to change the sheets on the bed and get some sleep.

With the apartment in order, I took out the trash to the shoot, then headed back inside and looked out the window. The protest had been broken up. A few demonstrators sat on the sidewalk in cuffs, their faces bloody, while the police chased the other stragglers away. I opened the window once again to air out the apartment and hoped the violence had remained on the street and hadn't oozed into our building.

It was time to fetch Ringo.

I hurried next door to Charles' apartment, who happened to be a war vet himself and suffered from some mental issues, but I'd never asked him for the official diagnosis. It simply wasn't my place. What I did know was that spending time with Ringo helped calm him, and he loved taking care of our cat when we were out of town. I wondered what he thought of the demonstrations? Did I want to ask, or would that only upset him?

After knocking gently so as not to distress him—loud noises often did—I waited patiently for him to answer. Chances were high he was home as he didn't go out much. Oftentimes he asked Donna and me to pick up a prescription or groceries for him, and he had other friends who dropped by on a frequent basis, but I'd never formally met any of them. Honestly, I found that quite strange. Yet, I'd never questioned Charles about it. Live and let live was my motto. If Charles didn't want his friends acquainted with me, that was fine. He was kind to us and loved Ringo like his own. We helped each other and I had no reason to stick my nose in his business.

"Charles?" I yelled, then knocked again.

I pressed my ear against the door and thought I heard voices. Perhaps the television? Then Ringo's distinct meow came through. The cat sounded like he was right on the other side of the door.

"Hi, Ringo!" I called, hoping Charles would hear me. "You okay, buddy?" The cat meowed again, and I once again rapped my knuckles on the wood. "Charles?"

Maybe he'd gone to sleep? He'd often complained that he was up at all hours of the night due to his mental issues from the war. When he did sleep, he'd told me it was like he was dead.

I knocked one final time. "Charles?"

My only response came from Ringo and I figured Charles couldn't hear me over the television.

With a sigh, I tried the knob and found the door unlocked. I stepped inside and called for him once again as I scooped up Ringo. "Charles, it's Patty! I just came for Ringo!"

A John Wayne movie blared from the television perched on a small table in the living room, but no one sat on the sofa to watch it. A desk sat in the corner piled high with newspapers and books. The smell of something burning also caught my attention, and I hurried into the kitchen to find a pot on the stove, the ingredients caked to the bottom. At one time, it may have been chicken soup. After removing the pot, I turned off the burner. At least it hadn't caught fire.

An IBM Selectric typewriter sat on the kitchen table with a stack of papers next to it. I picked one up and after glancing over a few paragraphs, I realized Charles had been writing a memoir of sorts, but he couldn't spell worth a darn.

"Where's Charles?" I asked Ringo as I stroked his head, worry now sitting heavily in my chest. The man may have had mental issues, but he'd never have forgotten food on the stove.

Gunshots went off in the living room, causing me to gasp and just about jump out of my skin. "It's that stupid television," I muttered, shaking my head. Hurrying over, I turned off the T.V. and an eerie silence fell over the apartment. A couple of sirens wailed in the distance, and I heard the neighbors walking down the hallway.

Yet, something was wrong. I could feel it in the chill that traveled up my spine and the goosebumps that crawled over my arms.

Holding Ringo close to my chest, I slowly walked toward the bedroom. The door lay half-way open, and I stared at it a moment. "Charles?" I called.

As I pushed open the panel, my heart thundered and my knees weakened. A scream escaped me when I found Charles lying on the floor, a knife protruding from his stomach, his blank gaze staring at the ceiling.

Chapter 2

RIGHTFULLY SO, MY PLANS FOR A QUIET EVENING flew out the window when I found Charles dead.

I immediately hurried back to my apartment and called the police, and because so many were downstairs breaking up the protestors, they arrived within a minute or two.

With shaky hands, I lit a cigarette while the cop sat down on the opposite side of the couch from me. I didn't usually smoke but finding a man dead with a knife in his stomach seemed to be a good reason to fire one up.

"My name's Officer O'Malley," the policeman said curtly. With his thinning hair and the fine lines around his cold blue eyes, I pegged him to be in his forties. A huge beast of a man standing well over six feet and weighing in over two hundred pounds. He took out a pad of paper and I imagined he'd seen a lot of horrible things in his career to be so brusque. "I'll be sitting with you until the lead detective arrives. What's your full name, miss?"

"Patricia Byrne," I said, stroking Ringo's back as he sat on my lap. He must have realized I needed him for moral support.

I had always been terrible with names. Someone could introduce themselves to me and I couldn't recall their name fifteen seconds later, especially when I was nervous. I'd started to give people little nicknames to help me out—usually something that described their personality, a physical trait, or while flying, what they were drinking. Sometimes it took me weeks to remember a moniker, but my little trick seemed to help.

Ogre O'Malley.

"And how did you know the deceased?" he asked.

"Well, he was our neighbor," I said. "He watched our cat for us when we were out of town."

"We?"

"Yes. My roommate Donna and me."

"What do you do that takes you out of town?" he asked, jotting down some notes.

"We're stewardesses for Cross Country Airlines."

He glanced up at me, then shook his head and I had an idea of what he was thinking. Stews had a reputation as easy party girls, and for some, like Donna, that was true. Even the airline's advertising played up this rumor. However, I had become a stew simply because I wanted to travel, see new places and experience new things. I wasn't quite ready for marriage, and college wasn't an option for me.

"And can you tell me how you managed to find Mr..."

"Mr. Bernard," I replied, blowing a cloud of smoke above me. "Charles Bernard."

"Why were you in his apartment?"

"Like I said, he babysat our cat for us. I'd just gotten home, and I went to retrieve Ringo. I noted his door was open, so I walked in, thinking he might not have heard me with the television on."

"His door was open? As in ajar?"

I shook my head. "No. Unlocked."

He furrowed his brow as he continued to take

14

notes. "Did you often barge into his apartment like that?"

As I stubbed out my cigarette in irritation, I wished I had poured a glass of wine. "I didn't barge in on him. I knocked many times and thought he couldn't hear me. When I realized the door was unlocked I went in and found him."

The cop seemed to be making something nefarious out of my innocent actions, and it grated on me. However, I'd been taught to respect authority, so I'd hold my tongue. Instead, I smiled sweetly, hoping to hide my annoyance.

"Okay. What can you tell me about him?"

What did I know about my neighbor? Actually, quite a bit, and I didn't like speaking of him. It felt like gossip to me and it was rude to gossip about the dead.

"Anything you can tell me may help solve the case," Officer O'Malley said gently.

A knock sounded at the open door, and I looked over his shoulder to find another man dressed in a brown trench coat and matching fedora, looking like he'd just walked off the set of *Dragnet*. "May I come in?" he asked as he held up a badge.

I nodded and motioned for him to enter. Ogre

O'Malley stood and turned to him. "Her name's Patricia Byrne. She found the stiff next door. Seems pretty shaken up about it."

With a sigh, I shut my eyes for a brief moment. They talked about me as if I wasn't in the room, and my frustration grew.

"Thanks. I'll take it from here," the guy in the trench coat said, then patted Officer O'Malley on the shoulder as he took the notebook. He smiled, then filled the cushion on the couch O'Malley had just left.

"I'm Detective Peterson," he said, removing his hat and setting it on the coffee table. "I'm truly sorry you had to see that horrible sight next door."

"Thank you," I murmured, grateful that he appeared to be a little nicer than the hardened O'Malley.

Pleasant Peterson.

"Can you tell me how long you've known the deceased?"

"We moved in about six months ago," I said. "He was very friendly and quickly fell in love with old Ringo here. He was aware we traveled a lot, so he asked if he could keep Ringo company while we were out of town. It worked out great for all of us.

Ringo didn't get angry at being left alone and Charles had a friend."

"Just curious... how do you know Ringo doesn't like to be left alone?"

I met his stare, the color of his eyes reminding me of chocolate milk. "He tears apart clothing or pees everywhere when he's mad. We came home to destroyed garments quite a few times before Charles offered to help us out." When I glanced around the apartment, I realized my bras and nylons were still strung all over. My cheeks heated in embarrassment. How many strange men would be casting their gaze on them?

The detective chuckled and shook his head. "I'm glad you found a solution to that issue."

"Me too."

"I know this is hard, but what can you tell me about your neighbor?"

Over his shoulder, more police milled about in the hall. For the first time, tears welled in my eyes, and gossip or not, I had to help find justice for Charles.

"He was a veteran," I said, wiping the tears tracking down my cheeks. "He served in Vietnam and he told us he had some mental issues because of it."

Detective Peterson reached into his coat pocket and handed me a kerchief. I unfolded it and dabbed my face. If I didn't get my emotions under control, my eyes would be puffy tomorrow, which the airline frowned upon, regardless of the reasons.

"Did he say what those were?" he asked, his voice soft. His kindness only brought more emotion.

"I'm sorry," I whispered, the tears streaming down my cheeks.

"There's nothing to be sorry for," he said. "You've been through quite a trauma. We can sit here until you're ready to talk."

It took a few moments for me to regain my composure while I listened to the hustle out in the hallway. Finally, I could meet his gaze again. "I think I'm ready."

"Excellent," he said with a smile. "Tell me about Mr. Bernard's mental issues."

"He really didn't go into a lot of detail, but he did tell me he didn't like loud noises. He also said he didn't sleep well."

"Did he seem strange? Or dangerous?"

"Not at all. He was a lovely neighbor."

The detective scribbled notes down on the pad. "Did he have a lot of friends?"

"I've seen a few come and go," I replied as I

rubbed Ringo's ear. "There was one man I saw more frequently than the others, but I don't know his name. Charles was also seeing a woman... Karen."

"What's Karen's last name?"

I shrugged and shook my head. "I'm sorry. I have no idea."

"What about people he didn't get along with? Did you ever witness him arguing with anyone?"

"Oh, yes," I replied. "A man in this building... I believe he lives on the second floor. He's been terrible to Charles and they've exchanged some pretty heated words."

"What about?"

"The war," I said, sighing. "The man downstairs is a huge war protestor. Charles is... was a veteran who believed in the war and was honorably discharged. That neighbor called him awful names."

"Like what?"

"He told Charles he was a baby-killer, that he had the blood of women and children on his hands, that the war was un-American. Things like that."

"And what did Charles say?"

"That he was fighting for the country he loved

and doing his duty. It got pretty heated a few times, and they almost came to blows."

"Wow. What's the man's name?"

I couldn't remember my nickname for him. "I'm not sure. Donna and I usually tried to make ourselves scarce whenever we saw them arguing. I think he lives in 2C."

He flipped back through his notes. "Donna being your roommate?"

"Yes."

"And where is she?"

"She's working," I replied, dabbing my eyes once again. "I'm not sure when she'll be back."

"What about your other neighbors on the other side? Have you seen them today?"

"No."

"And their names?"

"Dusk and Rainbow."

Detective Peterson stared at me a moment, then asked, "Are they hippies?"

I nodded. "They're nice people, but yes, they're members of the so-called counter-culture."

As he scribbled more notes, I studied the action in the hallway over his shoulder. So many police had arrived for Charles' death.

"I was told there was an anti-war protest outside this building today. Is that accurate?"

"Yes. And then the pro-war people showed up, and then the police."

"Do you think it's possible that someone came into the building and killed Mr. Bernard?"

"I... I don't know. When I got home, the super said they'd lit a trashcan on fire in the lobby."

"Protesting the war?"

"I guess. He was grumbling about the anti-war demonstrators, so I assume that's who he meant."

"Interesting," the detective said. "How does your super feel about the Vietnam conflict?"

"Well, we've never discussed it, but based on what he's said, he believes it's important that we continue with it."

"Hey, Boss?" a policeman called from the hallway, and both of us turned to him. "We also found some unsigned divorce papers."

Peterson glanced over at me. "Were you aware he was getting divorced?"

I shook my head, gasping in shock. "I had no idea!"

"He never mentioned a wife?"

"Not once! He only talked about Karen and

introduced me to her once. Never did he mention a wife."

"Do you think Karen knew he was married?"

"I don't know. Like I said, I only met her once."

More racket came from the hallway, and Ringo jumped from my lap and ran into the bedroom. No wonder he and Charles got along so well—neither of them liked loud noises.

Three men wheeled out a gurney that I hadn't noticed come in. And just like that, Charles was gone. Tears welled once again and I couldn't believe I'd found myself in such a situation.

Detective Peterson smiled again and fished out a business card from his coat pocket. "Please give me a call if you think of anything that can help us solve this murder."

As he shut the door behind him, I stared at the card. Murder. My neighbor had been murdered.

For the first time since finding Charles, I suddenly felt very afraid. I glanced around the apartment as voices filtered in from the hallway. How long would the police be going through his things? Had Charles been killed while I was at home, dancing around to the Beatles and doing my laundry? Or had he been dead for some time? If I had gone over earlier, could I have also been a victim, or perhaps even stopped the killing?

Suddenly feeling very sick to my stomach, I hurried to the bathroom and splashed cool water on my face.

As I stared at my puffy eyes in the mirror, I couldn't help but wonder... was I safe in my own apartment?

Chapter 3

BEFORE I ENTERED THE AIRPORT, I TOOK OUT MY Mary Quant compact and studied my reflection once again, grimacing at my puffy eyes. Honestly, it was expected. After the police had left, I'd cried more from both fear and losing a friend. Sleep hadn't come easily and I'd woken at every sound, convinced someone had come to shove a knife in *my* stomach. I'd never been so happy to see the first slice of daylight through the curtains, even if it revealed a cold, wet day.

"You can do this," I whispered to my tired eyes, then shoved the compact back into my bag and smiled.

As I made my way through the airport, I grinned and nodded at those who stared at me.

The first time it had happened, I'd found it quite disconcerting. The looks ranged from outright hatred to lust. Thankfully, a senior stew had explained it to me. The men who ogled us wanted to bed us. The women who glared either hated us because they were afraid we'd steal their husbands, or they secretly wished they could have our carefree lives. Once I understood, I had quickly become used to it and now just accepted it as part of the job.

"Patty!"

Turning around at the sound of my name, I found Captain Dorchester jogging to catch up to me. A nice man with a lovely wife, he was one of the few who didn't get touchy-feely with the stews. When I'd first met him, I'd dubbed him Doe-Eyed Dorchester because he had the kindest, warmest brown gaze I'd ever seen.

"Captain Dorchester!" I said as he approached. "What a lovely surprise!"

"I haven't seen you in a while," he said as we continued our walk to the airline personnel staging area. "We haven't been on any flights together recently."

"That's true. Where are you off to today?"

"Seattle, then on to Chicago. What about you?"

"New Mexico to Dallas with a layover and back here tonight."

"Busy day for you."

"Yes."

"I haven't seen Donna around for a while either. How's she?"

Everyone knew we lived together. "She's fine. Honestly, I haven't seen much of her either. Our schedules have been off."

Tears pricked my eyes as I thought of Ringo being left home alone. I hadn't known how to write Donna a note stating that Charles had been murdered, so I'd simply jotted that he was unavailable and hoped I'd catch her to explain before she saw it on the news. Since Donna hated watching anything but Hogan's Heroes (she had a mad crush on Bob Crane) or the Ed Sullivan show, I had faith I could get to her before she saw anything official about it. Besides, I'd lived through the night knowing about the murder, and I didn't want to do that to her. It had been terrifying.

We hurried through the door off-limits to the general public and down the concrete stairs. When we arrived at our airline's staging area, we were met with a flurry of activity.

"I'll see you later, Patty," the captain said,

flashing me a grin. "Hopefully we'll get to fly together soon!"

I waved as we parted, him going over to the captain area while I strode to where the stews had been lined up. After dropping my case, I fell in line next to a woman named Beth. Busty Beth. We exchanged hellos and waited for the head stew, Linda, to make her way down the line as she inspected each of us.

"Geraldine, your eyeliner is a little off on your right top lid. Please fix it. Victoria, you definitely need a trim. I can see your split ends from here. Judy, I can tell you've lost weight. Nice job." The critiques and accolades continued as the head stew gave us the once over.

"Beth, honey, you need to get on a diet." I glanced over at the woman next to me. She didn't look heavy to me, but I didn't have Linda's critical eye. "Your buttons are about to burst."

In order to get the job, stews had to be pretty, between five-foot-two and five-foot-nine and weigh no more than one-hundred-and-forty-pounds. Our weight was checked weekly and we suffered these inspections at the beginning of each day before we flew. I appreciated the airline wanted us to represent them in a very specific way, but every time a girl broke down into sobs as Beth looked to be on the brink of, anger roiled through me. We were all more than a pretty face and a pert bustline.

"I'm already so hungry!" she complained. "I'm trying to lose, but I feel like I'm starving!"

"Maybe you need to take up smoking," Linda said. "It does wonders for your appetite, dear."

She moved her gaze to me and crinkled her nose. "My goodness, Patty. Your eyes are so puffy!"

"I know," I said, staring straight ahead and not meeting her stare. "When I got home yesterday, I found my neighbor murdered. It was quite upsetting."

All the girls gasped and turned to me.

"My word!" Linda said, holding her hand over her heart. "What a horrible thing."

"Yes, it was. So, please forgive me. Hopefully, I won't be discovering any further dead bodies in the future and you won't see my puffy eyes."

"Of course, dear," Linda said, placing her hands on my waist, then patting me. The gesture probably looked as if she consoled me, yet I knew she was only doing a sly girdle check.

At no time was there a question of if I was okay to fly, and I was fine with that. I needed to be working, to get my mind off the horrid sight of Charles' body. If Linda had sent me home, I wouldn't have known what to do.

She turned to the group. "Ladies, you have your assignments for the day. Remember, Friday is weigh-in, and some of you are coming close to that number where I have to fire you, so please watch your snacking. Smile and be kind and generous to everyone on the plane. You never know, girls... your future husband may be flying with you today!"

This was one of the things the airline advertised in their hiring. A few of the girls squealed, but Beth and I exchanged glances that indicated neither of us had any desire to meet a husband. However, I did have a three-hour layover in Dallas, and hoped to sneak away and see some of the sights.

We all picked up our bags and moved along to our planes. "Looks like I'm with you," Beth said, walking next to me.

"Very cool!" I said, excited to work with her. We got along famously.

"Do you think I'm getting fat?"

I glimpsed over at her as we crossed the tarmac. On second glance, the buttons on her blouse did appear to be a little strained, but no more than usual. "That's silly," I said. "I think you look great."

"You're always so sweet, Patty," she replied with a sigh. "Thank you."

Once we'd put away our bags and done a quick inspection of the plane, we waited for our passengers. Beth greeted them as they embarked while I stood at the back and helped people put their luggage up and get settled. Our head stew, the one in charge of the flight, had yet to make an appearance and Beth and I whispered a bet that it was Penny. Party Penny. She'd been with the airline a few years and was an even worse party girl than Donna. Penny had her sights on a captain and she wasn't shy about letting everyone know.

"Can I get a gin and tonic before we take off, sweetheart?" a man asked as he sat down and I pushed his briefcase into the luggage rack above him.

"Of course, sir. Just give me a moment."

As I raced to help people into their seats, fetch cocktails, and have friendly chats with those boarding, men lit up cigarettes all around me. As a fairly new stew, I was forced to work in the back of the plane where the smoke seemed to be the worst, which I didn't mind most of the time. However, Mr. Gin and Tonic was a chain-smoker, so the air became quite polluted fairly quickly.

After gathering the empty glasses and getting ready for takeoff, I walked the aisle for one last inspection of my passengers to ensure they all wore seatbelts and I hadn't missed picking up a glass. I found an unruly little boy, about four years old, who simply didn't want to sit down. His mother also seemed to be at her wits' end with him. I did note she wore a lovely shade of coral lipstick that I'd never seen before.

"Good morning," I said, squatting down so I was eye-level with the little terror. "Is everything okay here?"

The mother shook her head, and I noted her eye bags were worse than mine. "He won't sit down."

I smiled and looked at the boy. "What's your name?"

"Mikey," he said, still refusing to sit and jumping up and down.

Monster Mikey.

"Well, Mikey, my name's Patty. I'm a stewardess on this flight, which means I have special access to parts of the plane where the passengers can't go."

His eyes widened. "Really?"

"Yes. Would you like to see some of those areas?"

"Yes! Yes! Yes!"

I laughed and shook my head. "Well, here's the thing. I need you to be a big boy and sit down with your seatbelt on and mind your mom. If you can do that, then I'll take you up to see the captain."

He thought about my offer for a brief moment, and I worried he wouldn't take me up on it. Finally, he nodded and sat down. "Okay. I'll be good and listen to my mommy."

"Excellent," I said, standing. "I'll let the captain know he's going to have a very special visitor once we get in the air."

"Thank you," the mother said. "I appreciate your help."

"Of course," I replied, laying my hand on her shoulder. "Glad I could assist. If you don't mind, I love your lipstick. Is that Mary Quant?"

"Thank you! No, it's a new shade just released by Yardley."

"It looks lovely with your complexion. Excellent choice."

I continued my inspection and then took my seat for takeoff while Party Penny's voice filled the cabin with instructions on what to do if the plane crashed. I'd been so busy I hadn't noted her arrival. Although I was trained in saving lives in such an event, I really believed there wasn't much to be done if the plane went down but to pray.

Once the captain gave us the all-clear, I jumped into action. I took orders in my section, then prepared my tray for their delivery. Even at ten o'clock in the morning, the alcohol flowed freely among the businessmen, the majority of our clientele. Once everyone had been served, I called the captain and received permission to bring Mikey up front.

"Are you ready?" I asked, noting he still sat in his chair with his seatbelt on. "It looks like you've earned your trip to the cockpit."

"Yes!" he shouted, trying to wiggle free from his confines.

"The captain says you can't yell," I said as his mom unlatched his seatbelt. "So let's talk quietly, not in loud voices, okay?"

He hurried out into the aisle and I took his hand to lead him up to the front of the plane. I held on tight to keep the little terror from running. When we reached the cockpit, I knocked gently and wasn't surprised to find Penny on the other side.

"Who is this?" she asked, eyeing the kid.

Monster Mikey.

"This is Mikey, and he's been such a good boy I

told him he could meet the captain and see the cockpit."

"Wonderful!" Penny exclaimed. "We love rewarding nice children, don't we?"

"Yes, we do."

The captain turned and waved to me, then said, "Come on in, Mikey! I'll show you around."

"I'll watch him," Penny said as the kid scooted by her. "Where is his seat?"

"22-D," I replied, realizing she was dismissing me. She wanted the captains to herself, which was fine with me. I'd get a head start on the clean-up.

As I smiled, chatted, and poured drinks for my customers, I was able to forget about Charles for a little bit, and some semblance of normalcy returned. Yet, the idea of going back to my apartment alone scared me to death.

Who had killed Charles? And more importantly, why? Had it been random, and if so, were Donna and I their next potential victims?

Chapter 4

AS MY DAY WORE ON, I KEPT A CUP OF COFFEE ON hand while my energy waned considerably. I sighed with disappointment as we landed in Dallas only to discover I wouldn't be doing any sightseeing during my layover due to the torrential rain. I spent my layover in the airport with more hot coffee. At least I had a book to keep me company.

Once everyone was off the plane, Beth and I disembarked before Penny and the rest of the crew. We smiled as we walked through the airport and waved at the little kids.

"My feet are killing me," she said between gritted teeth. "Do you want to grab a quick bite? I'm on my way to Chicago in an hour."

"Sure," I said. "I'd like that." Anything to keep my mind off the murder.

We stopped at one of the restaurants and were seated right away. I ordered more coffee and decided on a turkey sandwich with a side-salad. That would definitely keep me tied over until I got home, and maybe even until the next morning.

"I'll have the burger and a slice of cherry pie," Beth said to the waitress. "Actually, make it two pieces of pie."

I held my tongue and drank some coffee. Beth's job may be on the line, but it wasn't my place to police her about her weight.

We had a wonderful lunch gossiping about our co-workers and she shared her mother had been sick, which caused her a lot of stress.

"What can I say?" she said, stabbing her fork into the second piece of pie. "I'm a stress eater."

I sipped my coffee as she devoured the cherry goodness.

"Tell me what's going on with you, Patty. You said something earlier about your neighbor being killed? That sounds absolutely horrible. Were you close?"

Frankly, I'd rather hear about her sick mother than discuss my murdered neighbor, but on the other hand, perhaps it would be good for me to talk about it. It sat around me heavily, like an uncomfortable, wet blanket.

"We were friendly," I said. "He watched our cat while we worked. He was a good guy."

"Well, who do you think did it?"

The question caught me by surprise. Why would I consider who had committed the murder? Wasn't that the police's job?

"I... I don't know."

"You have to have some idea!" Beth said. "Think about it! Who do you think killed him?"

"Well, he was a private man," I said. "As I mentioned, we were friendly, but not close."

"I don't believe you, Patty! Think!"

As I recalled my interview with the detective, I realized I did have a suspect list, and my heart rate picked up as my excitement grew. "Well, there was an anti-war protest going on. Someone could have snuck upstairs from that, especially since a garbage can was lit on fire in the lobby. Charles, my neighbor, was a veteran."

"Oh, my goodness. Why would a bunch of anti-war protestors kill him?"

"As I said, he was a veteran. You know how they treat veterans."

"Yes. It's disgraceful. Who else besides a name-less, faceless demonstrator?"

"One of our neighbors downstairs is an anti-war protestor. He and Charles have had words in the past."

"That sounds like a promising lead. At least it's not some faceless demonstrator. Who else?"

"Well, the police asked me about friends and people he dated. There are a few guys that come around, and he was dating a woman named Karen. But then, they also found divorce papers in his apartment."

Beth gasped and sat back in her chair, shaking her head. "He wasn't divorced and dating someone else?"

"Yes."

"Oh, my. That's absolutely appalling."

"Agreed. I was shocked to learn about it."

"And you don't know the friends?"

"No," I said, shaking my head. "It was almost like... like Charles didn't want to introduce them to me."

The thought sent a chill down my spine because I hadn't realized it before. Had Charles been protecting me from them? He'd been open to me meeting Karen, but not any of his friends. If so, why? There was only one that really stuck out in my mind, and I had to admit, he was a fairly unsavory character. With long, black, greasy hair down to his waist and his glazed over eyes, he'd never struck me as particularly friendly, but more predatory than anything.

"You've got quite the suspect list," Beth said. "You could probably solve this case. You found the body and you had a birds-eye view of his life."

"I don't know about that. I have no idea how to go about solving a murder."

"Well, according to Perry Mason, you need a motive. Why would someone want to kill him?"

"Maybe Karen found out that he was married?" I said with a shrug. "Maybe the wife learned about Karen?"

"Oh! Maybe he owed a friend money?" Beth said, her eyes wide with excitement.

"Or it could have been the protestors," I speculated.

"Perhaps even the nasty neighbor," Beth said. "Lots of motives, Patty, and very exciting."

"That's all well and good, but it doesn't mean I'm qualified to solve a murder."

Beth rolled her eyes. "Why not? Is it because you're a woman?"

And frankly, once I gave it some thought, that did have something to do with it. All the police had been men, and they'd been in charge.

"Men aren't smarter than us," Beth continued. "A lot of them think they are. Some even believe women aren't good for anything but having babies and homemaking. Things are changing though, Patty. You just watch."

Feminism. There definitely was a wave of women who were demanding equality to men. They wanted to work where men worked, to have the same opportunities as men. Of course, I did as well, and it was one reason I'd become a stew. I didn't want marriage and babies at that point, but my job prospects were limited, especially without a college education.

"No one has a better understanding of Charles than you," Beth continued. "Except, maybe Karen, the girlfriend. But from what you've told me, you weren't really involved in his life."

"He watched Ringo for us," I reminded her. "I wasn't involved at all."

"So your cat was involved in his life," she replied. Interesting and true. Ringo knew more about the man than I did. "*You* weren't. You were a spectator. You know all the people involved, yet you can remain impartial about everyone. Who do you think did it?

"I have no idea," I huffed. "And I wouldn't know where to start to figure that out."

Beth glanced at her watch, then grinned and stood, throwing a couple bills on the table. "That should cover my share. To solve a murder, you need to talk to people, Patty. That's what Perry Mason does. You're so cute and personable, you'll have no trouble getting people to open up to you. Start with Karen though. Always start with the skirt, because women are just as awful as men on a basic, biological level, but men think of us as delicate and incapable of violence. They're wrong."

As Beth strode away, I stared at the tabletop. What had that business about violence meant? Was she speaking from experience? I'd been angry enough to become violent before, but I'd never acted on it. Had she?

What if I did take steps to solve the killing? At least I wouldn't feel like a sitting duck when I was home. I allowed myself a brief fantasy of bringing the murderer to justice, being interviewed on television and receiving accolades from the police department and my airline.

The headlines would read, *The Stewardess Who Discovered the Murderess*.

Well, if it was Karen. Or the wife.

What would it hurt to talk to Karen? Even my neighbor? I could report anything I learned to Detective Peterson. Or, I could make myself a target for sticking my nose where it didn't belong.

———

THE DINNERTIME CROWD was always rowdy with businessmen having finished their meetings for the day and heading on to their next stop, or home. They usually arrived on the plane tipsy from the airport bar and proceeded to drink more with their dinners. The more alcohol they consumed, the more obnoxious they became. Sometimes I found it slightly amusing until someone threw up or passed out so hard, I couldn't rouse them at the end of the flight. Of course, there were also those who got a little handsy, thinking that no one saw them in the dimly lit cabin.

As my passengers filed in and down the aisle, I smiled and greeted them, hoping the flight back to San Francisco would be non-eventful.

A businessman grinned at me, and I could tell

by his easy manner he'd had a great day. Probably closed a big deal. A couple boarded, and the wife fidgeted, her brow pinched in worry. A nervous flier. I spoke to her a few moments and assured her that I would take great care of her and airline travel was safe.

My hopes for a dull flight were quickly dashed when I saw the man teetering down the aisle holding onto the back of the seats as he eyed me, making absolutely no attempt to hide his appreciation of my looks. No doubt, he would be trouble.

"Hey, honey," he slurred. "Can you help me find my seat?"

"Of course, sir. Let's take a look at your ticket." I assisted him to his chair. "Here you are!"

"What's that?" he asked, pointing at the cushion.

There was nothing on the seat. I bent over to where he pointed to get a closer look, yet I still didn't notice anything out of the ordinary. The chair appeared to be in good shape.

When I straightened up, I caught him staring at my backside, and I realized he'd wanted me to bend over to see my skirt ride up my legs. Pig. Mr. Pig it was.

"Take a seat, sir," I said through gritted teeth. "What can I get you to drink?"

"Vodka and soda."

When I brought back the drink, he'd passed out. Normally, I'd be happy about it, but I also worried he would toss his cookies if we hit any turbulence.

After takeoff, I prepared the chicken meals for my section, garnishing each tray with a white rose. It was a shame most of them would end up in the garbage, but some of the men actually brought them home to their wives or girlfriends. Every now and then, I'd receive one as the passengers debarked at our destination. This usually went along with a request for a phone number or a dinner date, which I declined. A lot of the stews were on the search for husbands, so they frequently dated passengers.

The flight remained uneventful and I kept an eye on Mr. Pig, who snored loudly. At least the jerk still breathed.

Exhaustion railed through me and I walked down the aisle one last time to check on everyone. One passenger in particular had caught my eye. Dressed in a white button-down shirt and a black suit, he wore his dark hair short. His green gaze had been kind the first time he'd asked me for coffee.

Throughout the flight, he'd studied some papers, even while he ate. I'd dubbed him Mr. Coffee.

"Can I get you a nightcap, sir?" I asked quietly so as not to disturb anyone else.

"No, thank you," he said, slipping off his glasses, his Texas accent thick. "I could use another cup of coffee, though."

"I was just thinking the same thing," I said. "I'll get a fresh pot brewing for us."

On my way back to the coffee machine, I took a couple more orders for drinks. Once I had everything situated on my tray, I headed down the aisle.

Mr. Pig was still out cold, thankfully. Yet, just before I passed him, I noted him shifting in his seat out of the corner of my eye. His leg must have moved into the aisle because the next thing I knew, my tray of drinks went flying and my chin hit the floor. I groaned at the impact and pain radiated through the front of my body—everything from my ankles to my forehead hurt.

Chapter 5

"LET ME HELP YOU UP," A MAN'S VOICE SAID FROM above me. Strong hands held my shoulders and gently pulled. Once I was upright, I found Mr. Coffee had been my savior.

"I am so sorry," I said, glancing at the mess in the aisle while smoothing down my skirt. At least it hadn't ridden too far up and given everyone a show. My co-worker, Ruth, rushed from the front of the plane and began dropping cleaning cloths to soak up all the liquid and handing out others to passengers who'd gotten wet, all while smiling profusely and apologizing.

"No worries," he said, smiling. "Are you okay? It looks like you have a scratch on your chin."

My injuries could wait. I'd made a terrible mess

and needed to clean it up. I looked over at Mr. Pig, and his leg *was* stretched out into the aisle, but he still slept soundly, unaware of the chaos he'd caused.

I stepped back to pick up a glass and almost fell over again. Pain shot through my ankle as I tried to catch my balance.

"Uh-oh. You may have a sprain there," Mr. Coffee said. "Let's get you back to your chair and I'll take a look."

"I need to help her clean up," I said, pointing to Ruth.

He glanced over his shoulder, then back at me. "It's fine. None of the glasses broke and you can barely walk. Let's get you seated and I'll give her a hand."

I began to argue again but putting weight on my ankle made me decide otherwise. After taking off my heel, I hobbled to my chair with his help.

"Stay here," he said. "I'll be right back."

With a sigh, I shut my eyes. I should have been more careful. Sleeping drunks had a tendency to sprawl out and I knew that. I'd been *warned* about it in training. How in the world was I going to get home if I couldn't walk? Once we landed, I could get a wheelchair to the cab area, and then stagger up to my apartment.

"Okay, he said, returning. "Everything is cleaned up. May I take a look at your ankle?"

"I guess so," I replied. "Are you a doctor?"

"No, but I've had some medical training."

He dropped to his haunches in front of me and gently probed the tender area with cool and smooth hands. "I don't think it's broken," he said. "Probably a minor sprain."

With a smile, he met my gaze. "I'm Bill, by the way. I should have introduced myself before grabbing your foot."

Even in the dim light, his eyes were so green, they reminded me of pictures I'd seen of the ocean in some parts of the world. "That's okay. I really appreciate your help. I'm Patty."

"Are you okay?" Ruth said, coming around the corner. "That was quite a spill!"

"Yes," I replied. "I think I'll be fine. Probably sidelined a few days, but Bill here says that he doesn't think it's broken."

"Oh, thank goodness! How are you going to get home?"

"I'm not sure."

"I'll help you," Ruth volunteered. "After you get checked out in medical at the airport."

A few moments later, the captain announced our impending landing. Ruth handled everything for me, and I'd owe her big time. Once the passengers departed, she helped me down the aisle and into the waiting wheelchair, which in turn took me to medical.

Mr. Coffee, or Bill, had been right... nothing but a sprain.

THE NEXT DAY, I sat on my couch eating a bag of potato chips and watching reruns of *Dragnet*. My stomach would revolt against the chips, and so would my waistline, but I didn't care. The doctor had ordered me to take a few days off, and more if need be in order to get my ankle back into shape. I had nothing but time, so I toyed with ideas on what to do with it.

When I'd arrived home the previous night, I hadn't been as frightened as I had been after Charles' death, but I still woke with every groan and sound in the apartment complex. Beth's words kept recycling through my head. *You could probably solve this case. You found the body and you had a birds-eye view of his life.*

I didn't see any harm in asking a few questions if I saw the people on my list of suspects. After all, I looked pretty harmless, especially being on crutches. That also made me an easy target if I spoke to the actual murderer and said the wrong thing, but I tried not to think about that part.

When Sargent Joe Friday caught his man on the television and received accolades, I quickly made up my mind. I was going to try to solve Charles' murder. Perhaps that would lead to me becoming one of the first women detectives on the police force. Would my father be proud of that? He certainly didn't like me being a stew.

Just over a year ago, I had become terribly excited to learn of the opportunity to interview for the position. I'd imagined a glamorous life of meeting movie stars and seeing the world. When I arrived home and told my parents of my plans, my mother burst into tears and my father turned so red with fury, I thought he would have a heart attack. *No daughter of mine is going to become one of those girls!* he had yelled. Frankly, the dramatic scene had only made me more deter-mined, so I interviewed and got the job. I didn't tell them until the day before I was to leave for training.

My relationship with them was still strained. My dad didn't speak to me for months, and now, the conversations were short and curt. My mother had no interest in hearing about my job. I hadn't become one of the party girls they feared I would, but they still assumed I had embraced the hedonistic lifestyle the media portrayed.

Perhaps a change in careers would please them and mend our relationship. Or maybe they'd think of me as a woman who just wanted to push my way into a man's field for the attention.

A knock sounded at my door, and I rose to open it, then teetered over on my crutches. I'd been using them a few hours and my armpits already hurt.

I opened it to find one of Charles' friends—the one with the long, greasy hair. "Can I help you?"

He stared at me a moment with glazed eyes. "Have you seen Charles?"

I almost blurted out that he was dead but decided to see if I could fish for a little information instead. "Um... no. Is there a problem? I'm sorry, I don't believe we've ever been introduced."

"I go by Wayne. He owes me money."

"Ah, yes," I said, nodding, as if I understood

completely. "It's nice to put a name with the face, Wayne. He owed me money as well once when he didn't have enough to pay his electric bill."

"He owes me for something else."

"What's that?"

He hedged a moment and glanced both ways in the hall as if he wanted to be certain no one overheard our conversation. "Weed," he whispered. "If you ever need any, I'm the guy you want to call." I smiled and nodded, hoping to hide the shock that railed through me. Charles had done *drugs*? "It would help a lot with your ankle," Wayne continued.

"T-thank you," I replied. "It's not too bad. Just a really mild sprain. I'll be up and around in no time after a bit of rest."

"That's good. Can you tell Charles I topped by?"

And there was the catch. Did I tell him Charles was dead, or simply play it off like I didn't know?

Wayne looked a little seedy, but he seemed pleasant enough, and it would probably be a good idea to let him know he wouldn't be seeing any of the money Charles owed him. "Well, I'm afraid I have some bad news."

"What's that?"

I pursed my lips together and hoped I wasn't making a huge mistake. In my gut, I didn't think Wayne was dangerous. If he'd killed Charles, then why come back to the scene of the crime looking for money? That simply didn't make any sense.

"Charles was killed."

That unfocused stare didn't leave me for a very long moment. Then, he glanced from Charles' door, and back to me. To my utter surprise, tears welled in his eyes and quickly tracked down his cheeks. "He's dead?"

"Yes."

"He survived 'Nam, and he's dead? How?"

"He... he was murdered."

Wayne placed his palms on the side of his head as if his thoughts would seep out his ears, and shut his eyes.

"Are you okay?" I asked, truly concerned. I hadn't expected such a reaction from a hardened drug dealer.

"Charles was my friend," he whispered. "How do you know he was murdered?"

"I found the body."

A string of inappropriate curses fell from his mouth and the tears continued. His chest rose and fell in labored pants as if he couldn't get enough air while he slowly spun in a circle. Wayne wasn't a murderer, but he did seem on the verge of some sort of attack. "Would you like to come in for a moment?" I asked.

He nodded and I moved aside so he could enter. Ringo eyed him from the kitchen and then ran for the bedroom. Either the cat didn't appreciate having his personal space invaded or he didn't like Wayne. Ringo had been present when Charles had been murdered, so the cat may recognize the killer. Is that why he ran? Because he'd watched Charles die? Had I made a terrible mistake in inviting Wayne in?

After he took a seat in the living room chair, I hesitantly sat on the couch. I couldn't imagine the devastation on the man's face being faked.

"We served together," he whispered as he wiped his eyes, his left knee quickly bobbing up and down. "Dang it. I never cry."

"I didn't know you were in the service," I said.

"It's not something I tell everyone about," he said with a sigh. "I don't want any trouble."

I recalled the anti-war protests and the violence that followed, and I understood. "Why did Charles smoke marijuana?" I asked, still trying to recover from the shock of that discovery. I had never smelled it coming from his apartment and he always seemed to have his wits about him.

"Nightmares," Wayne replied. "It helps with the nightmares. The crap the doctors give us don't work but weed does."

"Nightmares?"

"War is ugly," Wayne muttered, then swore again. "We've seen things no one should have to see. It stays with us."

I couldn't imagine the atrocities. The news always gave us a fairly sanitized version of the war, and I didn't even like watching that.

"I'm... I'm sorry, Wayne," I said, at a complete loss for words for the crying man in my living room.

"Me, too," he said, standing. "I guess I'm out my money and my weed."

He seemed to have aged a decade as he walked over to the door. His shoulders hunched and his feet shuffled against the carpet. The sound of the panel closing seemed to reverberate around the room like a gunshot.

As I stared into space and replayed my conversation with Wayne, my sympathies for the man, and for Charles, rose. Obviously, the nightmares were the mental issues he'd spoke of—his memories terrorizing him as he tried to sleep. I wouldn't have heard it as our apartments were mirror images, putting our bedrooms far from each other. However, I wondered if the neighbor on the other side of Charles heard him often. I'd have to pay Mrs. Wilson a visit and get her take on the sad situation.

I rose from the couch and teetered on my crutches as I struggled to find my balance. "Darn things," I muttered as Ringo sauntered back into the living room. "Hopefully I won't need them more than a day or two."

When I heard the key in the door, I turned to see Donna sauntering in carrying a bottle of wine and her overnight bag. "Lucy, I'm home!" she yelled in her worst Desi Arnaz accent, then kicked off her heels. When our gazes met, she furrowed her brow and her smile faded. "What the heck happened to you?"

Chapter 6

"I tripped over a Mr. Pig on the plane and took a spill," I said, limping my way over to her. "How was your flight?"

"Oh, my goodness," she replied, drawing me in a tight embrace. "Did you kick him between the legs?"

"Of course not," I said with a laugh. "I wanted to, but I refrained."

"Your resistance is impressive. Nice rug burn on the chin, by the way. Let me help you over to the couch. Good thing I brought home some wine."

Even though it was barely noon, she poured us both a glass and sat down next to me. She smoothed a hand over her blonde bob and her blue eyes twinkled with happiness and mischief.

If I had to describe Donna in a word, it would be something like *tornado*, or *whirlwind*. A party stew to her core, she lived for laughter, drama, and men. I loved being with her simply because she was so different from me, and we giggled like no one's business. She was the trailblazer, the one who garnered the spotlight wherever she went, and I was the one in her shadow who basked in pieces of her glory as she took over a room. I was fine being second fiddle when we ventured out together because 1 always thought living Donna's life would be absolutely exhausting.

"Where have you been?" I asked as she handed me mine.

Her eyes widened and she grinned ear-to-ear. "Patty, I got to go to France."

I gasped and envy washed through me. "Are you kidding me?"

"Nope. I saw it all. The Louvre. The Arc de Triomphe. Le Eiffel Tower! All of it!"

"Oh, my gosh. Was it as amazing as it looks in the brochures?"

"*Mais oui! Très belle!*"

I shook my head and sipped my wine. "How in the world did you land a spot on a plane to Paris?"

Both of us had graduated from stewardess

school around the same time and started where all the newcomers do: in the back of the plane. International travel was something reserved for the more senior stews. While I longed to be promoted to the front of the plane, Donna traipsed around the world. It didn't seem fair in the least bit.

"How do you think I did?" she grinned mischievously. I rolled my eyes, knowing the answer.

"You slept with a captain?"

Donna threw her head back and laughed, then reached out and touched the tip of my nose. "Bingo, my dear! After, I just happened to mention how much I wanted to see Paris, and he pulled some strings for me. Next up, I'm heading to see Big Ben! Or maybe the elephants in Africa!"

I did envy her, but I wasn't like her. I'd wait until I'd done my time in the rear of domestic travel and move up the ladder without compromising myself.

"If he asked, I'd marry him in a heartbeat," Donna said with a sigh. "He's such a gentleman. When we were in Paris, he took me to a few fancy restaurants and walking through the streets with him was so romantic. The weather was beautiful… sunny with a slight breeze. The food, the wine… it was such a great trip. I was sorry to have it end."

"Where does your captain live?"

"Seattle. We met in the airport in Utah a couple of weeks ago and hit it right off. I kept running into him during our travels, and in Boston... well, you know the rest. It's been magical."

Donna would love nothing more than to find the right man and settle down into a stable life. Unfortunately, she also thought every man she met was the right one and gave her heart away far too quickly. I'd always thought, deep down, Donna was terribly lonely and her need to be the center of attention was her way of fighting that loneliness. Perhaps it had something to do with the bits and pieces of her childhood she'd shared with me—a father who traveled all the time and a mother who would rather spend her days with a bottle of gin instead of her daughter.

"Is he single?"

Her grin faded as she shrugged. "I didn't ask, and he didn't tell. He wasn't wearing a ring, though, so I took that as a no."

I sighed and shook my head. "Not to be a downer, but you need to start asking, Donna. It's not fair to the wives. Think if you were in their shoes."

She nodded absently as her cheeks tinged pink,

but I knew she wouldn't discuss the subject any further. We'd already talked it to death.

"What's going on here?" Donna asked, glancing around the apartment. "Where's Ringo? Is he with Charles? You know, I think that cat may like him more than he likes us."

A quick change of subject to put her back in her comfort zone. "No, Ringo's here. He just went into the bedroom a little while ago."

On cue, the tabby stalked out and meowed, then jumped onto Donna's lap.

"There's my favorite boy," she whispered as she stroked his back. "You're the best boy ever. Even better than the captain who got me to Paris."

I snickered as she whispered her sweet nothings, but a heavy feeling settled in my chest. She obviously had no idea what had happened to Charles since she'd been jet-setting in Paris. Delivering bad news was such a bummer, especially since she was still on a high from her amazing trip.

"There's something I need to tell you," I said, setting down my glass on the coffee table.

"What's that?"

"Charles is dead."

Her eyes widened as she stared at me for a long moment. "Well, don't beat around the bush or anything," she said. "Oh, my goodness. What happened, Patty?"

"He was murdered."

"Murdered?" Donna whispered. "Are you kidding me?"

I shook my head.

Donna placed her hand over her mouth in surprise. "Did I lock the door? I better check." She handed me Ringo and ran over to examine the lock. "Who did it?" she asked as she returned to the couch and the cat immediately curled up in her lap again. He always wanted the attention of the one who had been gone the longest.

"The police don't know. I was the one who found him."

Donna stilled for a moment, then shook her head and poured more wine into her glass. "Start from the beginning. Tell me everything. This is just... horrible."

After I completed my story—everything from the demonstrators to my fear of being in the apartment—I waited for Donna to comment.

"I feel awful for Charles," she said. "That's a terrible way to go. I wonder who did it?"

"Well, I don't think it was his friend with the long, greasy hair. His name's Wayne, by the way."

"Why not him? I didn't really know him, but he always looked a little rough to me."

"He was here not too long ago," I replied. "He cried like a baby when I told him. And if he did do it, why come back to the scene of the crime? Why not stay away and keep off the radar?"

"That's a good point."

"Wayne said Charles suffered from nightmares from the war because of the things he saw when he served."

Donna shook her head and sighed. "That's awful. I'll tell you this: I wish I was still in Paris. Things here are downright depressing."

"I know."

"Did the police give you any indication on who they thought did it?"

"No. They asked me a lot of questions about people who knew Charles."

Donna sipped more wine and stared off into space. After a moment she asked, "Have you talked to Mrs. Wilson? To see what the cops said to her?"

"I haven't. I was actually about to hobble over there right before you came home."

"Let me change and freshen up," Donna said. "We'll go together."

Fifteen minutes later, we stood in front of Mrs.

Wilson's door and Donna knocked. We waited a few seconds, and then she answered.

"What a surprise!" Mrs. Wilson said, her face brightening up with a smile. "What can I do for you girls?"

Mrs. Wilson was in her sixties, a sturdily built widow who loved hearing stories of our travels. Donna had once said Mrs. Wilson lived vicariously through us. I only hoped I would be in as good as shape when I reached her age.

Unfortunately, she didn't get out of the building much except for her weekly trip to the salon to spruce up her gray bouffant and her monthly bridge meeting. Yet, she did like hanging around in the lobby downstairs and chatting with our super and the other residents, and claimed she got her exercise by climbing the apartment stairs.

"We wanted to talk to you about Charles," Donna said, leaning down and giving the woman a hug, who didn't stand an inch above five-foot-one.

"Oh, what a terrible thing," Mrs. Wilson said, her eyes widening when she noticed my crutches. "Come in. My goodness, Patty, what in the world happened to you?"

"A pig tripped her," Donna said.

"A pig? As in a police officer?"

"No, a different kind. A drunk and handsy customer," I clarified as I moved inside. "It's only a light sprain. I should be back on my feet in no time."

Once we'd gathered in the tidy living room, Mrs. Wilson smiled again. "Would you girls like some coffee or hot tea?"

"No, thank you," I said. I'd always liked her apartment because it smelled like sugar cookies. The pea green sofa and aqua blue chairs were from the fifties, but still in great shape. A black and white picture of Mrs. Wilson and her husband sat on top of the spindly-legged television and as always, I couldn't tear my gaze from it. Taken the day they were married, Mrs. Wilson stared at her husband with such love and hope shining from her eyes, my chest ached. She was an attractive woman, but in her youth, she'd been absolutely stunning with long, blonde hair and a megawatt smile.

We'd moved in after her husband had passed, and she'd told us bits and pieces of their lives together. They'd raised two children, the boy becoming a doctor while the girl went into teaching. She talked of her husband with longing and sometimes her eyes became misty. His death had been quick—a fall down the apartment stairs. I hoped to one day find someone who touched my soul that way, but not now. And I certainly wouldn't find him while shlepping drinks on a plane, no matter what the airline advertised.

I noted a new picture had been placed next to the wedding shot—two blond children staring adorably into the camera. Baring a slight resemblance to her, I guessed they were her grandchildren. The apartment had always seemed very homey to me.

"We're actually drinking wine," Donna said. "Want to join us?"

"Oh my. Drinking in the middle of the day. How scandalous. I'd love to."

Donna rushed back to our apartment and returned a few moments later with a full bottle she must have retrieved from our stash. If I had much more, I wouldn't be able to maneuver on my crutches.

Mrs. Wilson took a long sip of the Chardonnay, then asked, "What's on you girls' minds?"

"Well, we were wondering if the cops gave you any indication on who killed Charles," I said.

She shook her head. "None. They sure asked a lot of questions, though."

"Same here," I said. "They asked me about everyone he knew."

"Yes! They were quite nosey."

I pursed my lips together to hide my laughter. Mrs. Wilson calling someone else nosey was the pot calling the kettle black. She loved to lurk and listen, claiming no one paid her much attention because she was old and seemingly harmless. If I were a betting gal, I would say she knew something about everyone in this building.

"So, what did you tell them?" Donna asked. "Did you give them any good information?"

"Well, yes, I did," Mrs. Wilson said. "I told them about that horrid Bob downstairs—that hippy who's always throwing insults at Charles about him being a war veteran."

"I mentioned him as well," I said. Although, I hadn't remembered his name, but that shouldn't come as a surprise.

"And the demonstrators outside… they became so violent! If one of them knew Charles was a veteran, they could have taken advantage of the chaos and slipped in the building, killed him, and left without being seen."

I nodded and drank my wine. Apparently, Mrs.

Wilson and I thought very much alike. "I also mentioned Charles' girlfriend, Karen," I said.

"Really? Why?"

"They were asking about who I saw coming and going from the apartment," I replied with a shrug. "I just gave them the names of people I knew."

"I did the same, Patty."

"So, who do you think did it?" Donna asked, setting down her glass and rubbing her hands together.

Mrs. Wilson smiled and took a sip of her wine. "Well, I don't like to gossip, dear, especially not about the dead. It brings bad luck."

"It's not gossip," Donna said. "It's… it's conjecture. An educated guess based on what you know about Charles and the people in his life."

"I couldn't. It's disrespectful." Mrs. Wilson shook her head.

"We won't say anything," I interjected. "Like you, we live alone, and frankly, I'm a bit rattled that our neighbor has been killed. I just want to know who you think I should avoid if I see them."

"Yes," Donna said. "We don't want to find ourselves in a dangerous situation. So please… who do you think killed Charles?"

Chapter 7

MRS. WILSON STARED AT US OVER THE RIM OF HER glass while she sipped her wine. "Oh, heck. How can I resist such two beautiful girls? You know, when you sit next to each other like that, you remind me of salt and pepper shakers."

Donna and I exchanged glances, and I realized Mrs. Wilson was speaking of our hair. With mine being black and Donna's being light blonde, I understood the comment.

"Tell us!" Donna squealed.

"Okay, but I'm trusting you girls not to mention my thoughts to anyone else. Do you understand?"

We both nodded obediently. My heart raced as I waited for her to give her opinion.

"I believe it was his wife," she said quietly.

"His wife?" Donna asked, obviously disappointed. "Really?"

"Yes. She's an absolute shrew."

"Tell us about her," Donna said.

"Well, she and Charles moved in right after my husband died. That was three years ago, bless his soul. Anyway, after they were settled, I went over to introduce myself. Charles had just been discharged and was kind to me, but I could tell he wasn't comfortable in his own skin. He was jittery, as though he perpetually drank too much coffee. That's the only way I can explain it, but it was much more than that. Something much deeper in his soul besides caffeine. It was never said to me, but I do believe he was having trouble assimilating back into regular society. I imagine coming from the jungles into an apartment wouldn't be easy."

Donna and I nodded in agreement. I listened intently as Mrs. Wilson continued.

"Claudia seemed pleasant enough in the beginning. A tall girl with a blonde bob and a nice disposition. She was always smiling, always had a kind word to say. I'm sure Charles' issues didn't make life easy for her."

"His friend, Wayne, said that Charles suffered from nightmares," I said.

"When did you see Wayne?" Mrs. Wilson asked.

"Earlier today."

Mrs. Wilson lowered her voice to almost a whisper. "He's a nice man, but you know he's a marijuana dealer, don't you?"

"Yes. He told me that and also said the drug helped Charles with his sleeping issues."

"Well, it didn't work very well if you ask me," Mrs. Wilson said. "It scared me to death, but I never said anything. I'd just lie in bed and pity the poor fellow. He sounded as if his soul was being ripped from his body."

"Why didn't you say anything?" Donna asked.

"What good would it do, dear?" Mrs. Wilson replied with a shrug. "He'd simply be embarrassed, and he couldn't control it."

We all sipped our wine, almost as if we were having a moment of silence for Charles and the demons that haunted him.

"Anyway, the man suffered and Claudia became... different. I heard her yell at him many times."

"About the screaming at night?" Donna asked.

"No. Other things. She called him lazy. Told him he was good for nothing. Maybe a year and a half after they moved in, she told him she was tired of working two jobs and supporting him. That he needed to find work."

"Well, that's understandable," Donna said. "I'd be upset too if my husband sat on the couch all day while I worked."

"I never asked, but I don't think he could hold down a job," Mrs. Wilson said, tapping her head with her pointer finger. "He wasn't right up here."

"What happened then?" I asked.

"Oh, my goodness. One day, maybe a year ago, they had a huge fight that went on for what felt like hours. I heard glass breaking, things being smashed in the apartment. Frankly, I came close to calling the police."

"Why didn't you?" Donna asked.

"Well, I probably should have. All I heard was Claudia, though. Charles was a man and could certainly protect himself from her. I felt it was best to ignore the whole horrible episode."

I tried to imagine calm, friendly Charles in such a relationship, but it was difficult. Love definitely appeared to do strange things to a person for him to put up with such barbaric behavior from his wife.

"After that, I didn't see Claudia," Mrs. Wilson continued. "A few days after the incident, Charles apologized profusely for her outburst and said it wouldn't be an issue any longer as Claudia had left him.'"

"That's really a sad tale," I murmured. Perhaps it was the wine, but I found the whole scenario absolutely heartbreaking.

"Yes, well, Claudia filed for divorce a few months later. Right around the time you girls moved in, if I remember correctly."

"The police said they found the unsigned divorce papers," I said. "I had no idea he was even married."

"I don't know this as fact, but it appeared to me Charles didn't want a divorce," Mrs. Wilson said. "I think he hoped Claudia would one day come back."

"What about his girlfriend?" Donna asked. "Karen?"

Mrs. Wilson shrugged. "Perhaps someone to warm his bed? I don't know, dear."

"I don't understand," Donna said. "What does a bad breakup have to do with Charles dying? Why do you think Claudia killed him?"

"Well, Charles' grandfather died a few months ago and left him quite a bit of money. Charles actually brought me flowers after he'd been notified, and he said he'd never have to work again. He also offered to take me out to dinner, but we never got around to it. The man had his issues, but overall, he had a good heart."

"And what about Claudia?" I asked. "Did Charles tell her about the inheritance?"

"I'm not sure, but I wouldn't doubt it. If so... well, you understand why I think she killed him."

The pieces of the puzzle slowly started coming together. Charles had come into money but hadn't signed the divorce papers for whatever reason. It didn't matter. He wasn't divorced when he died. Most likely, Claudia was the beneficiary of any estate Charles had. If there hadn't been a will, then most certainly by law.

"Do you know how much he received from his grandfather?" I asked.

Mrs. Wilson shook her head. "I don't. He said he'd never have to work again and he wanted to thank me for being such a good neighbor."

"He never brought us flowers," Donna said with a huff. "Were we not good neighbors?"

"Charles had a much longer history with Mrs. Wilson than he did with us," I said. "If he didn't like us, he never would have watched Ringo."

"Oh, he loved your kitty so much!" Mrs. Wilson said. "He adored that cat and appreciated you girls allowing him to watch him while you were on your travels. Don't think he didn't value your friendship."

Donna rolled her eyes, obviously wishing she had flowers instead.

"So tell me, where have you girls been off to?" Mrs. Wilson asked. "Anywhere exciting?"

"Not for me," I replied. "Before I was hurt, I went to New Mexico and then onto Dallas, where it poured rain. But Donna just got back from Paris."

"Oh, my word!" Mrs. Wilson exclaimed, her face lighting up like a Christmas tree. "How thrilling! Tell me everything!"

As Donna spilled the details on her short, but utterly fantastic trip, Mrs. Wilson sat in rapt attention while my mind wandered.

It sure seemed Claudia had a good reason to kill Charles, especially if he had enough money where he'd never have to work again.

But as I recalled the brutality of the crime scene, I wondered if a woman would be capable of such atrocities. Not only mentally, but physically as well. Could Claudia be strong enough to overpower Charles and lodge a knife in his stomach?

Or maybe she didn't have to subdue him with physical strength. Perhaps she'd romanced him with promises of getting back together in order to lower his defenses, and when she got close enough... BAM. Knife into the stomach of the man she had proclaimed she loved.

So very deceptive and cold, but definitely a possibility.

Personally, I couldn't imagine committing such a crime.

"What did Claudia do for work, Mrs. Wilson?" I asked, interrupting their conversation.

"Jeez, Patty," Donna said. "Way to ruin my story. I was about to tell her about my kiss at the Eiffel Tower."

"I'm sorry. I was just thinking about Claudia. I know she left Charles, but do you really think she disliked him enough to kill him?"

"Well, after the fight I heard, I'd have to say yes," Mrs. Wilson said. "Now, I'd like to hear about this kiss. How romantic!"

———

THAT NIGHT, I allowed Donna to sleep on the bed and I took the couch. There were two reasons: first, my foot felt much better propped up on the arm of the comfortable sofa. Second, she had a flight to catch and would need to use the shower before dawn. While she got ready, I hoped to keep sleeping.

My wishes were quickly dashed the next morning when I heard her moaning and groaning about a headache. Mrs. Wilson, Donna and I had finished off the bottle Donna had brought over. After coming home, she'd also drunk the one she and I had opened earlier in the day.

"I'm never drinking again," she said as she stumbled out of the bedroom and into the kitchen. "I'm sorry to wake you, but I need coffee."

"No worries. I was up." And I also knew she'd be partying once she arrived at her final flight destination.

She rummaged around the cabinets until she found the aspirin, then downed the pills with a gulp of coffee. "Do you want some coffee?"

"Sure. Thank you."

I sat up as she brought me a cup. "Where are you off to today?"

"To Boston, and on to Florida. I'll be gone a couple of days."

"I'll probably miss you," I said. "I'm hoping to be back at work by then."

We sat in silence as we drank our coffee and the sun rose, casting shadows in the kitchen. Raindrops began to hit the window, and Donna sighed. "I hope my hair doesn't frizz."

"I'm sure it'll be fine once you get in the air." Before then, I wasn't so sure because she did have a bit of natural curl in the blonde locks, and they did tend to kink in the San Francisco rain. Which meant she had the frizzies quite a bit.

"Ugh. I better get moving and finish packing," Donna said, checking the clock. "Could you please call me a cab?"

I gave her a thumbs up and when she walked back into the bedroom, I reached for the phone to make the call for her.

"Ten minutes!" I yelled when I hung up.

"Thanks!"

My thoughts had turned to the murder numerous times throughout the night, and I just didn't believe a woman could kill a man like that. Possibly, if pushed hard enough, women were capable of committing murder. But a knife in the stomach? It seemed so... barbaric to me.

But who had killed before and probably had experience with hand-to-hand combat? Wayne. If Charles owed him money and he'd been a little out of his mind from smoking marijuana, perhaps he'd used the skills he'd learned while serving in Vietnam.

It was something to consider.

"Okie-dokie!" Donna said as she emerged from the bedroom carrying a small suitcase. Her navy-blue uniform hugged all her curves. "Are the bags under my eyes too bad?"

I lied and shook my head. Whoever did the stew inspections would let her know the truth. "You look great. Have a fun flight."

"Always!" she sang as she sashayed out the door.

Standing, I put a little weight on my foot and was thrilled when I didn't have the shooting pain, but I grabbed my crutches anyway. No sense in over-doing it. I poured myself some more coffee, then sat down and watched The Morning News with Mike Wallace. When the show ended, I wished I'd never turned it on. The state of affairs was depressing.

With a sigh, I decided what to do with my day. Maybe read a book? Perhaps I could convince Mrs. Wilson to play some cards.

Promptly at nine, a knock sounded on my door. I teetered over to the door on my crutches.

The tapping came again. "Just a minute, please!" I yelled, then muttered, "so impatient."

I opened the door and my breath caught in my throat. The man grinned as I brought my hand to my mouth. It took a second

d for me to put a name with the handsome face, but then I blurted, "Mr. Coffee?"

Chapter 8

His smiled faded as his brow pinched in confusion. "I'm sorry?"

Dang it! He'd told me his name on the plane when he'd looked at my ankle, and of course, I couldn't recall it. "You're the person who helped me up when I tripped over that man's foot on the plane," I said. "You drank a lot of coffee."

His face lit up in recognition. "Of course. I thought I recognized you. Patty was your name."

"Yes!"

Once we'd recovered from the shock of the coincidence, I wondered why in the world Mr. Coffee was standing in the hallway outside my apartment. Running a hand over my hair, I wish I had been better prepared for his visit. I hadn't even brushed my teeth.

"*You're* Patricia Byrne?" he asked.

I noted he carried a green file folder. "Y-yes. What can I do to help you?"

What was his name? All I remembered was Mr. Coffee.

"Well, my name's Bill Hart," he said, pulling a badge from his jacket pocket." I'm a special agent with the FBI."

I stared at him a moment, wobbling on my crutches, almost falling to the floor. The FBI? What was the FBI doing darkening my doorstep?

"You look a little pale," Mr. Coffee said. "Are you okay?"

As I struggled to remember his name—darn it! He'd just told me!—I nodded absently, not feeling okay in the least bit. "What... why... why are you here?"

Did it have something to do with the airlines? The FBI dealt in national affairs, right? Had I done something illegal? I tried to think of my more recent flights, and nothing stuck out to me.

"May I come in, Ms. Byrne?"

I glanced from his badge back to him, a sinking feeling settling in my stomach. "What's this about?"

"Your neighbor's death. Unfortunately, I have to ask you a few questions since you were the one who found him."

My shoulders slumped in relief that it wasn't me in his crosshairs, but then guilt washed through me. I shouldn't be pleased about Charles' death. "Yes. I suppose so. Please, come in."

I shut the door behind him and motioned for him to sit on the couch, but I realized my blankets and pillow still littered the cushions. "I'm sorry about that," I said, trying to hustle over and remove them. As I leaned over to grab the blanket, my crutch fell and I almost lost my balance. Mr. Coffee grabbed my elbow and righted me. "It's fine," he said. "I can take care of this myself. Please, take a seat."

After hopping over to a chair, I fell onto the cushion. Instead of pushing the blankets aside, he folded them neatly and stacked them on top of one of the pillows, then set the other in front of me on the coffee table. "I don't want to tell you what to do, but you may be more comfortable with your foot elevated."

"Thank you," I said, setting my leg on the pillow. "I appreciate your help." Then, realizing my manners, I asked, "Would you like some hot tea? Maybe a coffee?"

"No thanks," he said, taking a seat. "Hot tea is... well, I can't say what I think of it in mixed company. I'm not a tea drinker."

"I can make coffee if you like."

"Really, I'm fine. Thank you." He opened his file folder. "As I said, I'm with the FBI and we're investigating your neighbor, Charles Bernard."

"Why is the FBI involved?"

"We believe it may be tied to a national investigation."

Interesting. "What national investigation?"

"I'm not at liberty to say."

"Why is that?"

I probably shouldn't be questioning the FBI on why they could or couldn't divulge certain information, but my curiosity had definitely been piqued.

"Well, it's... it's a matter of security."

"National security?" I asked, my mouth agape. "I find it hard to believe that Charles Bernard had anything to do with a breach of national security!"

"And why is that?"

I was about to say because my life was so boring, I simply couldn't have a neighbor that the

FBI had interest in. "I... I don't know. He just seemed so... normal."

But I realized my mistake there as well. Charles had been anything but normal. A married vet without a job who had come into money and who had a girlfriend and loved to babysit my cat? No, normal did not describe Charles at all. Perhaps chaotic would be a better word.

Mr. Coffee glanced at his papers. "It says here you found the body. Is that correct?"

"Yes."

"Could you tell me about that?"

"It should be in the report. I already told the police."

He smiled and pushed his glasses up his nose. "I know. I'd just like to hear it from you."

After I gave him the rundown on the happenings of that day, I sighed and wondered how many times I'd have to repeat myself.

"You didn't notice anyone around when you came upstairs from the demonstrations?"

I tried to recall if I'd seen anyone in the hallway. "I don't think I did. I was in a hurry to get inside my apartment because of the riots out in the street. The protestors had already set a garbage can on fire in the lobby. When I arrived at the building, my super said I should get upstairs for my own safety in case it spilled inside again. I was lugging my suitcase and focused on getting home. I didn't pay attention to whether anyone was in the hallway, but I don't remember seeing a soul."

"Okay," he said, jotting down a few notes. "I was also wondering if you noticed anything odd in the apartment when you found him."

I thought about Charles' place. Messy, but minimalistic. Nothing special. Maybe even drab. I couldn't recall what color his living room furniture was. "Not that I remember."

As he looked over his papers, he tapped his pen against the file folder. I admired his crisp black suit and white shirt. *Dapper* was the word that came to mind.

I was also incredibly curious about the FBI, and since I had an actual G-Man sitting in my living room, I decided to ask some questions. "Does the FBI employ women?" Maybe I'd skip becoming a cop and head right for the big agency.

"Sure. We have lots of secretaries."

"I mean in your position," I said, rolling my eyes. The last thing I wanted was to be trapped behind a desk. "Do you have a lot of women special agents?"

Mr. Coffee shook his head. "No. The position can be very dangerous. The bureau believes women wouldn't want to arrest people or practice self-defense."

I fisted my hand in my lap. Another man who assumed women only wanted to be married, have children, or sit behind a desk all day.

"What if one was interested in doing such things?" I asked, trying to keep my voice pleasant. "If a woman could prove herself, could she become an agent?"

"I'm not the one who decides those things," he said. "But personally, I think having women agents would be an asset to the FBI."

Tilting my head with a grin, I said, "And why is that?"

Mr. Coffee smiled at me. "Well, I do believe that women are just as capable as men."

How refreshing! His charms began to grow on me. If only I could remember his name.

"Getting back to the case, the police reports note that you had a couple of people you considered suspects."

"Well, I don't really know if they're suspects," I said. "They asked about people I saw coming and going from the apartment. I didn't actually say I thought any of them could have killed Charles."

"What can you tell me about Karen?" he asked. "The girlfriend."

"Not a lot," I said with a shrug. "I'd met her once or twice. She seemed nice enough, but I don't know if she's a murderer."

"There's a man in here you mentioned... It says you didn't have a name but he lives downstairs? He and Charles argued a lot?"

"Yes. He's an anti-war protester. Charles was a vet. Mrs. Wilson knows him, but I can't recall his name."

"Mrs. Wilson?"

"Yes. She lives on the other side of Charles."

"And you're friends with Mrs. Wilson?"

"Yes. We actually drank wine together yesterday while discussing the murder."

"Okay," he said, shoving papers into the file folder and closing it. "I know your ankle is hurt, but I was wondering if you wouldn't mind coming next door with me to take a look at the apartment."

A chill ran down my spine as I considered entering the space once again. "Why do you need me to do that?"

"I wanted you to take a look around with me, to see if you noticed anything strange or out of place."

At first, my reaction was no, but then I thought about it. I would be taking steps to find the killer and the sooner he or she was apprehended, the safer I'd feel.

"I'd be happy to," I said, standing as he also rose and handed me the crutches.

"How's the foot?" he asked.

"It's not too bad," I replied. "I think I'll be up and around in a few days."

"I'm glad to hear it."

As we exited my apartment into the hallway, he opened the door for me, then shut it behind us. After fishing out a set of keys from his pocket, he unlocked Charles' apartment and a blast of stale air tinged with a slight coppery smell smacked us in the face. It didn't seem to faze him as he stepped inside, and I decided to follow his lead. If I wanted to be taken seriously as a potential FBI agent, I better start acting like one.

They called people who worked with the agency G-Men. If I were able to secure a special agent position, would that make me a G-Woman?

First things first. The apartment.

I paused once inside and studied every nook I

could see. A wooden kitchen table sat to my right with a few papers neatly stacked on top of it. But instead of four chairs surrounding it, there were only three. I glanced around, searching for the missing seat, but couldn't find it. Perhaps it had been destroyed during Claudia's rampage Mrs. Wilson had mentioned.

The mustard yellow couch, looking worn and heavily used, faced the television. The carpet, a busy gold and brown pattern, had also seen better days and required a vacuum. Overall, the living space was somewhat tidy but in need of a cleaning—what I would expect from a man living alone.

"See anything out of place?"

I shook my head and crutched into the kitchen, promising myself I'd pay more attention to detail wherever I went in the future.

A couple of dirty dishes sat in the sink, including the pan with the burnt soup, and a few more were on the counter, drying.

"This smelled horrible when I first walked in," I said. "I was glad it hadn't caught fire."

"If you hadn't come in when you did, it may have. Then there'd be a lot more people hurt, or even dead. You potentially saved lives by entering."

I nodded, not feeling so awful anymore about coming in uninvited.

"Anything in here?" he asked.

Shaking my head, I realized I rarely left the entry when dropping off or picking up Ringo. I moved to the back bedroom and bit my tongue when I saw the bloodstain on the carpet. The image of Charles lying there played before my eyes clearly, as if he was still there.

Moving my gaze, I glanced at the unmade bed and bare nightstand. With the dusty outline, it looked like something belonged there but had been moved.

"What was there?" I asked, pointing to the spot.

Mr. Coffee opened the folder and pulled out the report. "Apparently, Mr. Bernard had a box there filled with marijuana cigarettes and bags of the substance."

"For his nightmares," I mumbled.

"I'm sorry?"

"I found out he had nightmares," I said.

"Who told you that?"

I turned to Mr. Coffee. "His friend, Wayne. He came by yesterday and said Charles owed him money and he wanted to collect."

He quickly shuffled through the papers, running

his finger down each one, his lips moving as he went. "I don't see anything in here about anyone named Wayne."

"I didn't know about him until after the police left."

Glancing around the bedroom once again, sadness washed over me. It had been a horrible way to die and I wanted to bring Charles' killer to justice.

"Does Wayne have a last name?" Mr. Coffee asked.

"I'm sure he does, but I don't know it," I replied with a shrug. "I do have his phone number."

"Excellent," he said. "I'll need to get that from you."

It was then that I realized I had information the authorities didn't, and it gave me an advantage. I glanced over at the G-Man and gave him my sweetest smile. "I'd like to help you in this investigation."

His eyes widened in surprise. "Really?"

"Yes. I can arrange for us to meet Wayne."

"It may be dangerous, Ms. Byrne. I couldn't put you in harm's way."

"Don't you worry about me," I dismissed. "And honestly, I'm not giving you a choice. I want to find

Charles' killer. It's important to me. You promise to let me tag along and I'll introduce you to everyone I know who could be involved. I promise you, Wayne will run for the hills if he sees you coming."

"And why is that?"

"Let's just say he deals in some illegal activities."

Mr. Coffee raised an eyebrow. "And you, Ms. Byrne? Are there any illegal activities I should be aware of?"

"No," I said with a sigh. "I'm just a stewardess."

"Who seems to want to be an FBI agent."

"It's crossed my mind," I said.

"May I call you Patty?" he asked.

"Of course."

"Patty, if I'm going to consider you assisting me in this investigation, I think we should become better acquainted. Would you care to join me for dinner tonight?"

Chapter 9

As I carefully applied my black eyeliner, I still struggled to remember Mr. Coffee's real name. Some FBI agent I'd be, running around, never able to recall the names of those I spoke to except for the stupid nicknames I gave them.

I interviewed Mr. Weasel Face and Mr. Vodka, sir. I think they're guilty. No, I don't recall their names.

That would go over really well with those in charge.

With a sigh, I ran my hand over my black bob and patted the ends to make sure the curl stayed in place. I had to admit, even with the scratches on my chin, I was having an excellent day in the looks department. My thick, soft, silky hair had curled to perfection and my makeup brought out the blue in my eyes. The drop waist yellow dress flattered my figure and also clashed with my black hair in a dramatic way.

As I studied my reflection, I decided I had two objectives for the evening: first, find out his name and remember the dang thing, and second, uncover why the FBI was interested in my neighbor's death. I didn't want to diminish Charles' early demise, but I didn't see it as being important enough for the FBI to bring out an investigator from Texas.

A knock sounded at the door promptly at six. I grabbed my crutches and hurried over to answer it. Mr. Coffee grinned at me from the threshold.

Dressed in a black suit, white shirt, and a tan trench coat with a matching fedora, he reminded me of the spies on television. Except he may be a little more handsome.

"Are you ready, or should I run down and tell the cab we'll be a minute or two?"

"I'm all set," I said, grabbing my gray overcoat and matching purse from the back of the kitchen chair.

"Excellent," he replied, helping me to slip into my coat. "I bribed a kid with a nickel to hold the elevator for us."

"How thoughtful," I said, smiling and meeting his gaze. "That thing takes forever."

"I figured as much. They always do in these old buildings."

Thankfully, I'd worn low heels to help keep my balance and prevent my chin from hitting any more floors.

Mr. Coffee stayed by my side as we made our way down the hallway to the boy leaning on the elevator door to prop it open. A cute little towheaded fella, about ten years old, who I recognized from a family living on the first floor.

"Thanks, kid," Mr. Coffee said, flipping him the coin. "Appreciate your help."

As we rode down to the main floor, I tried to think of a way I could broach the subject of me not remembering his name without sounding too ridiculous. I decided the direct approach would be best, even though it was probably the most absurd tactic.

"I have something quite embarrassing to ask you," I said, turning to him.

"There aren't any bad questions, Patty. What do you want to know?"

"What is your name?"

He stared at me a moment, his gaze narrowed

as if he was trying to figure out if I was being honest. "Bill Hart."

"Thank you," I said, glancing up at the numbers. With how slow the elevator traveled, one would think we had far more than three floors to descend. "I could only recall the nickname I gave you."

"Mr. Coffee?"

"Yes. Exactly."

Pursing my lips together, I lifted my chin and tried to remain dignified even though I felt like a silly little girl as he chuckled at my side.

"Just for future reference, it's probably not a good idea to accept a dinner date from a man whose name you don't remember," he said.

"Duly noted, Bill. Duly noted."

The doors slid open and we stepped out into the lobby. I glanced over at Nice Bill and smiled. With a grin, he opened the front door, from where I spotted the waiting cab at the curb.

"Where are we going?" I asked once we were situated. It had started to rain and the *ping, ping, ping* of the drops on the roof made for quite the racket.

"A steakhouse just down the street here. Have you ever been there?"

I shook my head. Unfortunately, I hadn't been

able to afford a meal at that place on my salary, nor had anyone I'd dated.

"My colleagues told me it's quite good," Bill continued. "That's one thing I miss when I'm away from home—a good steak."

The cab pulled over and Bill helped me from the backseat. The rain fell, and neither of us had bothered to bring an umbrella. Hopefully my eyeliner would stay in place and my hair wouldn't become too much of a mess.

Once inside, he removed his coat, helped me out of mine, and gave both to the woman at the coat check. He sighed as we were seated, as if relieved we'd finally made it to our destination.

White tablecloths covered every table and the lighting was quite dim. Definitely a restaurant for lovers, and I suddenly felt very out of place dining with Special Agent Bill Hart. I'd just learned his name, so I hoped he didn't think he'd be coming home with me after our meal.

"Would you like something to drink?" he asked.

"A glass of white wine would be lovely."

I marveled at the menu as the waiter came over and Bill ordered for us. Five dollars and ninety-five cents for a steak and potato! A pound of meat at the grocery store was right around ninety cents! A high-end eating establishment, indeed.

"Do you take all the people involved in your investigations to such nice restaurants?" I asked after we'd placed our orders and our drinks arrived.

"Only the pretty ones," he said with a wink, then sipped his gin and tonic.

My cheeks heated as I drank my wine. Admittedly, I loved compliments so I took a moment to bathe in his. "Tell me about yourself, Special Agent Bill Hart from Texas."

"Born and bred there," he said. "On a farm just outside Dallas."

"Brothers and sisters?"

"Two of each. I'm the oldest."

"And why did you want to become an FBI agent?"

"Well, I used to play cops and robbers when I was little. I hated being the robber. My whole life, I've wanted to catch the bad guys, so the FBI seemed the best way to do it."

"Why not a police officer?" I asked.

"I shot for the stars," he replied. "I wanted big things for myself."

Why bother telling him that I also wanted big

things for myself, but wasn't afforded the same opportunity as him?

"What about you, Patricia Byrne, stewardess extraordinaire? Where are you from?"

"My father was in sales, so I'm from a lot of places. We moved every couple of years, but I was born in New Jersey."

"Brothers and sisters?"

"I have one sister. She's older and married."

"Are you close with your family?"

As the waiter set down a basket of bread, I considered the question. Perhaps at one time I would have been able to answer with an unequivocal yes, but not now. "We used to be, but they don't... they don't like my job."

"Ah," he said. "And what made you want to become a stewardess?"

"I wanted to see the world," I said with a shrug. "I'm just not cut out for teaching or being stuck behind a desk, and college wasn't an option for me. I'm also not ready for a family and children. Maybe one day, but not now."

"Interesting. Most women your age are very interested in starting a family. What did your parents say when you told them you wanted to become a stewardess?"

That day was so fresh in my mind, and I felt physically sick whenever I thought about it. The screaming, the tears, the disappointment in their gazes... it all washed over me in one huge wave a guilt. "They weren't happy," I said, picking up a roll and taking a sip of wine. Who wanted to discuss such depressing things? Certainly, not me. Time to change the subject. "And what about your family? How did they react to you becoming an FBI agent?"

I imagined they'd be thrilled and very proud.

"They were pretty upset," he said. "The ranch has been in my family for generations and my parents thought they'd pass it to me since I'm the oldest, but the truth is, I hate ranching."

Both of us had disappointed our families by going our own way instead of down the path they thought best for us. "Maybe one of the younger children can take it over," I offered.

"I'm sure they will, but that doesn't alleviate any of the grief I caused."

The conversation came easily as we waited for our dinner. By the time my steak arrived, I was famished and almost forgot the second item on my agenda: why was the FBI bringing in an agent from Dallas to investigate my neighbor's murder?

"This almost tastes as good as back home," he said, slicing his steak into pieces. "Are you enjoying yours?"

"Very much so," I replied, even though I secretly worried about the calories. Girdles were bad enough to wear, but girdles that held in too many meals were the worst. The pinching and squeezing could become unbearable. Yet, I cleaned my plate. At those prices, I wouldn't leave one speck of food. I didn't want him to think of me as unappreciative.

"Would you like a coffee?" he asked when our plates had been cleared.

"Yes, thank you." Probably not the best idea since I'd be up late with the caffeine, but I didn't want the evening to end, and it was time to get down to my second agenda item. "So, please tell me, Special Agent Bill Hart... why do you have such an interest in my dead neighbor?"

"I'm with the FBI. I investigate things. Federal Bureau of *Investigations*," he said with a chuckle.

I grinned, but he wasn't going to dismiss my question so easily. "Murders happen every day in every city," I replied. "Yet, an FBI agent has flown in from Texas to probe into the killing of my neighbor. Forgive me, but it doesn't make any sense. Why aren't the police handling it?"

He stared at me a long moment, his smile slowly fading. As he glanced around the dining room and shifted in his seat, I realized I'd made him uncomfortable. Perhaps he wasn't used to people questioning him? After all, his role in life was *asking* questions, not *answering* them.

I almost apologized. Almost. Instead I bit my tongue and waited for an answer I felt I deserved. If he wanted my assistance in his case as he had claimed earlier in the day, then an explanation was warranted.

As he clasped his hands together on the tabletop and leaned forward, he studied my face for a long moment, and I wondered if I had a speck of bread stuck to my chin or lettuce in my teeth. "I suppose it won't hurt to tell you the truth, but Patty, this needs to be between you and me, okay?"

I mirrored his actions and nodded. To an onlooker, it most likely appeared we were in a deep, meaningful conversation. My heart pattered and the room became very warm. I was about to be let in on a government secret, but I attempted to set my features to neutral so as not to give away my excitement. "Of course. What is it?"

"I'm looking into Charles' death because I'm hunting a serial killer."

Chapter 10

"A serial killer!" I said, much too loudly. The table next to us glanced over as Bill hushed me. So much for me keeping my cool and harboring secrets well.

Bringing my hand to my mouth, I tried to recover from the shock. A serial killer? That option had never occurred to me.

"Please keep your voice down," Bill murmured as he smiled at the couple staring at us.

"I'm sorry," I whispered. "I just... I can't believe Charles was murdered by a serial killer."

The questions flew through my mind. How many others? Who did he think it was?

"He wasn't," Bill said, gripping my hand.

Confusion set in and I furrowed my brow. If he

wasn't murdered by a serial killer then why the investigation? "I don't understand. Please explain all this to me."

"Of course. But this isn't the place to do it," Bill said. "Can we go to my hotel or back to your place?"

Narrowing my gaze on him, I wondered if he was trying to get me into his bed?

"I promise I'll remain a gentleman," he said, as if he could read my thoughts. "This topic is sensitive and I shouldn't have brought it up in public."

And I should have kept my mouth shut instead of announcing our conversation to the restaurant. "We can head back to my apartment."

Bill asked the waiter to hail us a cab, then paid the check. When the hostess announced our ride had come, we made our way to the front door.

We remained quiet throughout the short drive, the rain once again pinging the roof. Pursing my lips, I wished I hadn't been taken by surprise and remained calm. Would he still confide in me, or was this the end of the road for my association with the charming special agent?

Once we were inside my apartment, I kicked off my shoes, shucked my coat, and fell onto the couch. The crutches made my armpits, ribs and arms hurt, and frankly, I wanted to be done with them.

"Let's get that leg up," Bill said, grabbing a pillow and setting it on the coffee table. Sitting down, he rubbed his hands together to warm them, and I was grateful he hadn't left.

"I'm sorry about my outburst in the restaurant," I said. "You caught me by surprise."

"I could see that," he replied, chuckling as he pushed his glasses up his nose. "It's not a big deal. I just think discussions about my work are better in private, and I should have remembered that before answering your question. Which is a good one, by the way."

"Tell me about this serial killer who didn't murder Charles," I said. "And how do you know he didn't?"

Bill leaned back against the cushions. "There wasn't any note left. The animal I'm hunting always leaves a note. The M.O. is the same—a knife to the stomach—but other things aren't right."

"What do the notes say?"

"Anti-war slogans, usually."

"How... how did you even end up in San Francisco? I don't understand."

"Police stations across the nation have been

notified to contact the FBI if they have a murder that fits within our parameters. I just happen to have a buddy on the San Francisco force who gave me a ring. I head up the task force that is searching for the serial killer, so I came out to look at the scene myself and to see my friend, Detective Peterson. Kill two birds with one stone, so to speak."

I crossed my arms over my chest and furrowed my brow. "Well, if it's not your killer, then why are you still here?"

"Detective Peterson asked me to stay around for a few days and see what I could find out," he replied with a shrug. "I had allocated three days to the investigation, so I told him I would."

"How many people has the man killed?" I asked.

"Four so far," Bill replied. "The last one was three weeks ago. Charles' murder would fit into the timeline of how long he waits between killings."

A chill of fear crawled up my spine. Bill's work terrified me on some level, but I also found it quite fascinating.

"But anyway, I'd like you to set up a meeting with Wayne tomorrow," he continued. "And have you accompany me there. I think he'll feel less threatened if I'm with someone he knows."

I shook my head. "He didn't kill Charles. It's a waste of time. And besides, we aren't friendly. I've seen him a few times in the hallway but I never knew his name. Charles never introduced us."

"Why is that?"

"I don't know. Wayne is a rough looking fellow. Perhaps Charles was... I don't know... somehow protecting Donna and me from him?"

"Do you consider Wayne dangerous? Why do you think us visiting him is a waste of time?"

"To answer your first question: maybe? If he was provoked? He is a vet and told me he'd done things in the war he wasn't proud of, which I took to mean violence. As for your second question, when I finally formally met him, he had no idea Charles was dead. He cried like a baby when I told him, which didn't seem like something a killer would do."

"Oh, you'd be surprised. Many come back to the scene of the crime to relive the rush, or if it was a crime of passion, be that anger or love, they return out of guilt. He could have been sorry he killed his friend, or he could have been faking the sadness. I think it's important to have a few words with him."

Recalling Wayne's tears, I didn't think he'd been pretending. They had seemed sincere to me.

If I ever killed anyone, I'd make a run for it to another country, preferably somewhere with a beach. Perhaps the Virgin Islands or Southern Mexico. I certainly wouldn't return to the crime scene.

But then, I didn't have the stomach to kill anyone, so perhaps my brain operated differently than a murderer's. At least I hoped so.

As I studied the man sitting in my apartment, I wondered if his mind worked the same as a killer's. In order to catch one, did he have to think like one?

"Could you call him and arrange something for tomorrow?" Bill asked. "Don't mention that you'll have an FBI agent tagging along, though. Just a meeting between you and him."

I hesitated for a brief moment, but then decided I still wanted to help Bill in the investigation. Reaching for the phone, I nodded. Wayne answered on the second ring.

"Hi Wayne. This is Patty Byrne, Charles' neighbor."

"Oh, yeah. Hey. What's up?"

Nerves tickled my belly as I twisted the phone

cord around my finger. "Listen, I was wondering if I could stop by tomorrow."

"Are you looking for product?"

"Yes," I said, grimacing. I hated lying and I didn't smoke pot.

"I can bring it by if you want."

Oh, heck. How in the world would I counter that?

"I'm actually going to be out running errands most of the day," I replied. "It would be far easier if we could set up a general time for me to meet you at your place, and then I'd come by."

Silence stretched on the other end, and I wondered if I'd pushed too hard. Or not hard enough. I had no idea what I was doing and was completely out of my element. I glanced over at Bill who nodded encouragingly.

"How about noon?" Wayne finally said.

"That's perfect," I replied with a grin. "I'll be by then. What's the address?"

As I grabbed a pen and jotted it down on the cover of a magazine, I noted my shaky hand. "Thank you, Wayne, and have a great night."

"Peace."

I hung up and sighed. "Tomorrow at noon."

"Excellent," Bill said, standing. "I'm going to

case the place tomorrow for about an hour before you arrive just to make sure it's safe. I'll meet you there."

"Do you want me to write down the address for you?"

He picked up the magazine and stared at it for a moment. "Nope. I've got it. I'll see you then. Good-night, Patty. Lock the door behind me."

I did just that and hobbled into the bedroom to get ready for bed. As I washed my face, I wondered if by offering to help find the killer, I'd put a target on my own back.

And was Bill really interested in me, or was he just taking me up on my offer to introduce him to all the suspects? How did I tell the difference?

━━━

THE NEXT DAY, while I dressed and applied a little bit of makeup, I tested walking around without my crutches. My ankle felt pretty good. To be safe, I slipped on my run-abouts—no heels for me—with a pair of pink capris and a white blouse with a matching sweater. The rain had begun to fall once again and the drafty apartment definitely held a bit of a chill.

I had slept well, but the question still played in the back of my mind: was Bill interested in me, or was I only a means to an end—catching a killer?

And no matter what the answer, did it matter? Yes, I found him attractive, charming, and very exciting, but he also lived in another state. Besides, I wasn't interested in a relationship. My goal was to see the world. I needed to do my time in the back of the plane and move up the ladder.

I took a cab to the address Wayne had provided. When the driver pulled up in front of an old warehouse, I couldn't help but wonder if I'd either written it down incorrectly, or he gave me the wrong one. People moved in and out of the building, so at least it wasn't abandoned. Perhaps it had been renovated into apartments.

As I exited the vehicle, I glanced around for Bill. I found him on the other side of the street standing under the awning of a Chinese Food restaurant. His stare narrowed as I limped toward him.

"How's the foot?" he asked, his gaze sliding over to the building.

"It's getting better. I can't wait to get rid of these crutches, but I didn't think now was the time."

He checked his watch. "Let's head inside. It's noon."

My assumption that the building had been reno-vated into apartments had been correct. We found Wayne's on the first floor, last door on the left.

Bill nodded and stood to the side with his back against the wall so that when Wayne opened the door, he wouldn't see the agent. Raising my hand, I tapped on the wooden panel that reminded me of a barn door.

My heart thundered as I waited for Wayne to answer.

Footsteps sounded inside, and the panel slid to the side. I smiled when Wayne came into view, his hair still a greasy curtain.

"Hey," he said. "Come on in."

As he stepped to the left, I entered. I heard the door beginning to close behind me, but then Wayne yelled.

I turned to see Bill holding up his badge in one hand while shoving Wayne with the other. "Let's take a seat, partner," the agent growled as he pushed him toward the sofa.

I remained cemented to my spot, thoroughly stunned and unable to move. Bill handled the man so roughly, it surprised me. I supposed I should have expected to see that side of him sooner or later.

Wayne sat down on the old, tattered brown

couch and raised his hands to his shoulders. "What's the deal, man? I don't have any drugs on me."

"I'm not interested in your drugs," Bill said, standing in front of him. "I'm interested in the death of Charles Bernard and I want you to tell me exactly where you were the day he died."

I'd always been a big believer that a person could catch more flies with honey than with vinegar, and Bill seemed to be going pretty hard at Wayne.

"Get out of my apartment, pig."

"Not until you answer my question," Bill said, his tone low and deadly.

The two stared at each other for a long moment. Wayne became more agitated by the second, his hands shaking and his lips moving as though he had a conversation no one else could hear. He then shot up from the couch and pushed Bill, who lost his balance and fell backward on the coffee table.

Wayne ran for the door as I screamed.

I didn't know what to do. Let him go? Step out of the way? Try to stop him? If I truly had been Bill's partner, what would be expected of me?

I did the only thing I could think of: I stretched out my arm and tripped him with my crutch.

Chapter 11

Wayne landed face-first on the wooden floor. Bill struggled to standing, then ran over and stood over him.

"Nice work," Bill murmured as he leaned over and grabbed the other man's arm, hauling him to his feet.

Wayne glared at me and I smiled apologetically. "We need to get to the bottom of the murder," I said. "Please help us."

Once Wayne was back in position, Bill asked, "Why are you running?"

"Because you're a cop!" the guy yelled, blood trickling from his mouth.

"It makes you look guilty," Bill growled. "I may be a cop, but I just wanted to have a chat. Are you going to sit there and answer my questions like a good little soldier, or do I need to haul you down to the police station for an interrogation?"

I narrowed my gaze on Mr. Special Agent Bill Hart who was becoming less and less special with each passing moment. The conversation he'd claimed to want to have had quickly dissolved into something quite ugly, in my opinion.

"Fine," Wayne said with a sigh, his voice resigned. "Ask me what you want. I don't know anything about Charles' murder."

"Where were you that day?"

"I stopped by Charles' place in the morning to deliver his weed. He told me he didn't have the money, but he'd get it. We'd been friends for years. I knew him during the war, so he was good for it. He'd never scammed me before. I told him I'd be back the next day to collect."

Bill glanced over at me as if I could verify the account. "I was on a plane the day Charles was murdered," I said with a shrug. "I saw Wayne the next day."

"Yeah, man. That's when I came back to collect. Charles said he'd have the money then."

"What were you wearing?"

Wayne's gaze faltered for a moment and he

glanced around the room as if searching for an answer. "I don't know," he finally said. "Probably the same clothes I'm wearing now or something similar."

His too-big jeans were cinched at the hips with a belt and his tattered orange and red sweater had seen better days.

Did the fact he couldn't remember what he wore make him guilty?

Since the chase had been thwarted, I glanced around the drafty room that had once been a corner of a warehouse. The sofa where the two men talked sat against a blank brick wall. Directly in front of me was a kitchen area, and to my left lay the bed, a sink, and a toilet. The windows faced the alleyway. The space struck me as depressing at best, and in need of a deep cleaning. Charles' apartment looked pristine compared to Wayne's.

"Did you two ever argue?" Bill asked.

"Sure we did," Wayne said. "But we were army buddies. I always knew he had my back and I had his. It ain't easy being a war vet and it's easier to keep to ourselves. No one knows what we've been through. When Charles was killed, I lost one of my best friends."

With a sigh, I shook my head. How could Bill not see his innocence? It was so apparent to me.

"Why did he smoke marijuana?" Bill asked.

"The war," Wayne said, shaking his head. "It really messed with him. Gave him nightmares. It helped him sleep."

Bill crossed his arms over his chest and stared at him, but said nothing.

"Look... I didn't kill him, okay?" the man said, his arms at his sides. "I didn't kill my friend."

I believed him. His sincerity touched me deeply. In my eyes, he wasn't a suspect, but a man who lost a very close friend, possibly even close enough to be considered a brother. The bond they'd developed on the battlefield had been strong.

"Don't you be heading out of town anytime soon," Bill growled.

"I'm not going anywhere." Wayne leaned his head back against the cushions. "I've got nowhere to go."

Bill strode over to me and grinned, a direct contradiction to the man I'd just witnessed interrogating his suspect. "Ready to go?"

I furrowed my brow and nodded. How strange. A true Dr. Jekyll and Mr. Hyde.

"Sorry things got a little rough in there," he said

as we stepped onto the street. "Nice work with the crutch, though. You saved me from a foot chase."

"I thought you were going there to *talk* to him," I said. "Not badger him."

"Sometimes the only way you can get to these guys is to show dominance. And that's probably one reason women aren't in the FBI. It's hard to show dominance when you're physically small."

The declaration didn't sit well with me, but I nodded in agreement anyway. Could a woman be dominant over a man? I'd seen some flight attendants put a man back in his seat with nothing but a glare. Women had other ways to appear commanding without physical size.

"Care to share a cab with me?" he asked. "I'd like to also chat with Mrs. Wilson, Charles' neighbor."

"Thank you, yes," I said. Special Agent Bill Hart had lost some of his luster, but if he was paying for the ride, I'd take it.

He attempted to hail a cab a few times while I leaned against the building, but none stopped. Coming from Dallas, he'd probably have better luck getting a horse's attention.

Leaving my crutches up against the wall, I walked over to the street with surprisingly little pain. In the second lane, I noted a cab about a half-block away. As soon as the cars closest to us drove by, I stepped into the street and whistled, then pointed at the driver. He quickly moved over to the sidewalk and stopped for us.

When I turned to Bill, he chuckled and shook his head. "You continue to impress me, Patty."

He hurried over and grabbed my crutches and we entered the vehicle. Once on the road, I stared out at the city passing by and thought about our interview with Wayne.

I now regretted my offer to help Bill by introducing him to the people in Charles' world. He was being a rude brute, and I wouldn't allow him to treat others that way.

"I'll introduce you to my neighbor, but I would appreciate it if you were a little more polite to her than you were with Wayne," I said, not meeting his gaze. "She's a very sweet widow who won't tolerate being intimidated like that."

"You think I intimidated Wayne?" he asked.

"Yes," I said, turning to him. "I'm sure it's a requirement with certain subjects in your line of work, but it wasn't necessary with him."

"How do you know that?"

"Because I work with people," I replied. "I can

tell after a very short period of time what tone I need to take with someone. Wayne may have been afraid of you at first and tried to run, but if you hadn't been so pushy to begin with, I think we could have avoided the confrontation."

Bill stared at me a long while, then said, "You realize I'm a trained FBI agent, right? I was simply following the protocol I deemed fit to use on a drug dealer."

"I know exactly who you are. And your training is fine and dandy, Bill. I'm just saying I do believe things would have gone much smoother if you'd have been a little nicer. And I'm asking that you be pleasant to Mrs. Wilson. Frankly, after what I just witnessed, I'm hesitant to introduce you. I don't want your training and protocol to ruin my friendship with her."

Turning back toward the window, I hoped he realized I wasn't requesting a behavior change. I demanded it. Mrs. Wilson deserved better.

"I'll be on my best behavior with her, Patty."

AS I KNOCKED on Mrs. Wilson's door, I glanced over at Bill again. "Please remember to be polite. She's an elderly woman. Show some respect."

He rolled his eyes as she answered.

"Patty!" she said. "What an unexpected surprise! Who's this fine-looking fellow?"

"This is Special Agent Bill Hart of the FBI," I said. "He's looking into Charles' murder."

"It's lovely to meet you, ma'am," he said with a grin, taking her slender palm in his as his Texas accent suddenly became more pronounced. The heavier it became, the less intimidating he was, and I wondered why. Perhaps people linked a thick accent with friendliness? "I just need to ask you a few questions and I was hoping it would be a good time for you."

"Of course. Come in. Always happy to help law enforcement." Once we were seated in her tidy living room, she offered us tea.

"I'd love some," Bill said. "Thank you so much."

My goodness. Wasn't he pouring on the charm, now thicker than maple syrup.

"You told me you hate tea," I murmured.

"I do, but you said I had to be polite. She offered, so I took her up on it."

I sighed. Mrs. Wilson brought over a white porcelain tray lined with pink flowers and a matching tea pot and cups. "Sugar and cream?" she asked as she poured.

Bill glanced over at me and I realized he had no idea which combination would make the golden water more palatable.

"Both for me," I said, giving him a slight nod.

"Same here," he said.

As Bill settled back into the cushions, I watched him out of the corner of my eye. He sipped the brew and hid a scowl, but then smiled. "It's delicious, Mrs. Wilson. Thank you."

"What can I do for you two?" she asked.

"Bill is looking into Charles' murder for the police," I said. "He just wanted to ask you a couple of questions and requested that I accompany him."

"Oh, of course," she replied, her gaze firmly on Bill. "Such a shame. What can I tell you about it?"

"I've read your statement, so there's no need to tell me everything again. I just have a few follow-up questions."

Mrs. Wilson sipped her tea, staring over her cup expectantly.

"I was wondering if you saw Charles' friend, Wayne, around that day."

"Yes. He was here early in the day... I can't remember what time. Probably before noon, though, if my memory serves me correctly."

"And did you see him later in the afternoon?"

"I believe so, but I can't be certain. Patty said he stopped by the day after and she spoke to him."

As I picked up my cup, I tried to hide my surprise of finding an inconsistency in Wayne's story. He'd told Bill he'd never come back that afternoon, only the next day. My gaze slid over to Bill. Had he caught it as well?

The smile never left his lips and he sat forward as if everything Mrs. Wilson said was important and he had become enthralled with listening to her. He gave her the audience she seemed to want.

While working, I'd used similar tactics with chatty customers. A smile and nod even while tuned out did wonders to placate people, and I felt that's exactly what Bill was doing to Mrs. Wilson.

"Do you remember what Wayne was wearing when you saw him the day of the murder?"

She furrowed her brow and pursed her lips as she set down her teacup. "I can't be certain, but maybe jeans and a patterned sweater. That sounds about right."

Bill tipped back his cup and drank it in one long

swallow, then set it down. "Thank you for your time, ma'am. It's been greatly appreciated."

We stood and the three of us moved toward the door. I now used the crutches as a means of support, but also placed my full weight on my bad foot.

"Thank you again for speaking with me, ma'am," Bill said. "It's been wonderful meeting you."

We walked down the hallway in silence to my apartment. Ringo greeted us when I unlocked the door. As Bill shut the panel, I turned to him excitedly. "Did you catch it? The inconsistency?"

He nodded. "I did. Wayne said he wasn't here twice that day, but that sweet old lady says she thinks he was."

I slowly walked over to the couch without my crutches and sat down. "Why did you ask what he was wearing?"

"Because if I can get another witness in this building who says he saw Wayne here that afternoon wearing that awful sweater, I'm one step closer to nailing him."

Chapter 12

THAT EVENING, I STARED AT THE TELEVISION BUT didn't track what Lassie was up to. My mind swirled around Charles' murder, considering all the suspects and trying to figure out who'd killed him.

For some reason, the thought of Wayne being the killer still didn't sit right with me, but I couldn't peg as to why. Perhaps it was simply his demeanor. However, if the evidence, such as someone else seeing him in the apartment building late in the day of the murder, proved to be true, then he'd been caught in a lie and I would have to admit my hunch had been wrong.

There were still others on the suspect list that had been provided during police interviews who Bill needed to speak to. I didn't know if he'd ask me to accompany him, but I hoped he did. I found the work fascinating and I liked the idea of assisting him in solving the case.

When I thought I heard drawers closing in Charles' apartment, I stood and turned off the television to listen better. Our unit may not be situated so that we could hear Charles' screams at night, but we could certainly detect movement in the living room.

Yes. Someone was definitely in Charles' place.

I grabbed my crutch and stepped out into the hallway to find Mrs. Wilson staring at the half-open door.

"Did you hear someone in there?" I whispered.

She nodded. "Should we call the police?"

I'd had the same thought, but what if they didn't arrive in time to find out who it was? We'd miss out on this important clue!

"I say we go inside," I murmured.

Mrs. Wilson shook her head. "Are you crazy or brave?"

"Is there a difference?"

"Good point, dear. I do think we should call the police beforehand, though. Just so we know they're on the way."

"Okay. I'll wait here and make sure they don't slip out while you call."

I waited at the ready, my crutch over my shoulder like a baseball bat. My heart thundered and beads of sweat dampened my forehead. Crazy or brave? What a great question. I felt a little bit of both.

A moment later, Mrs. Wilson returned and I fully pushed the door open, realizing I should have called Bill as well. He'd want to be aware of this new development. Perhaps a stranger had simply broken into the apartment and this was all a big coincidence, or maybe it was the murderer. My hands trembled in fear at the thought.

As we stepped inside, I saw a figure going through the desk drawers in the living room carrying a flashlight to light their path. Tall and thin, I couldn't discern if it was a man or a woman, but I tightened my grip on my crutch.

Mrs. Wilson flipped on the lights and with a gasp, the intruder turned to us. A blonde woman who I guessed was Charles' wife glared at us—her hand over her heart, her gaze filled with cold hatred.

"Claudia?" Mrs. Wilson said. "What are you doing here?"

Clammy Claudia because of her frigid scowl.

"I'm looking for something."

"What would that be, dear?" Mrs. Wilson asked.

Claudia lifted her chin and crossed her arms over her chest. "I don't think that's any of your business."

"You don't live here any longer," Mrs. Wilson said softly. "So, being Charles' neighbor, I have to say that it is my business."

The two women stared each other down for a moment as I lowered my crutch and propped it under my arm. Claudia turned and opened another drawer as if we weren't standing mere feet away, watching her.

"What are you looking for?" Mrs. Wilson asked again. "Are you aware Charles is dead?"

"Yes. As his *wife*, I was informed."

"You left him, though," Mrs. Wilson said. "You may have been married on paper, but not in the eyes of God."

Claudia spun around and place her fists on her thin hips. "He wouldn't sign the papers!" she yelled. "I begged, pleaded and threatened him, and the lazy jerk still wouldn't sign!"

Threatened?! Had she followed through? Perhaps with a knife to the stomach?

"Well, the police took the divorce papers, if that's what you're looking for," I said.

Claudia's shoulders sagged, but then she narrowed her frigid blue gaze on me. "Who are you?"

"Charles' other neighbor. My name's Patty. We moved in after... after you left."

She studied me from head to toe, her mouth turned in disgust. "Were you the girlfriend?"

"Um... no. Just the neighbor. Charles used to babysit my cat while I was away."

Claudia rolled her eyes and leaned against the desk. "Away where?"

"I'm a stewardess, so I'm gone quite a bit."

"Figures," she muttered with snort.

"Excuse me?" I said, unsure what part of the conversation she was referring to.

"I couldn't get that man to change his clothes, let alone babysit anything or get a job. You, the pretty stew, moves in next door and he's bending over backwards to accommodate your stupid *cat*."

Not the way I saw it, but Clammy Claudia seemed to have a large chip on her shoulder where Charles was concerned. "He said my cat helped him with... his issues. It was actually a win-win situation for all of us."

"All of us?"

"Yes. Ringo, our cat, doesn't like to be left alone."

"That man's issues ran too deep for a cat to fix. Unless, of course, the cat poops marijuana."

I smiled sweetly, but Clammy Claudia sat firmly on my last nerve. "I can assure you that doesn't happen."

"Why don't you two nosey neighbors go back to your own places and leave me alone?" Claudia said. "I've got enough problems without you both staring at me."

"We called the police, dear," Mrs. Wilson said. "I wish you would have let me know you were coming over."

Claudia crossed the room in a flash and stared down at Mrs. Wilson, wagging her finger in the older woman's face. "Call them right now and tell them not to come!"

I expected Mrs. Wilson to wilt under the hatred directed at her, but instead, she pursed her lips and shook her head. "You're trespassing, Claudia. This isn't your home any longer."

"He's my husband," she hissed.

Mrs. Wilson crossed her arms over her chest. "Was. He *was* your husband. We'll let the police decide on whether you belong here or not."

Clammy Claudia's cheeks turned absolutely crimson as she glared at the small woman. "Are you threatening to hold me here until the police arrive?"

"I hadn't given it much thought," Mrs. Wilson replied. "But I guess expecting you to do the right thing—stay and talk to the police—would be assuming too much of you."

Even I winced at the blatant cut.

"Why do you hate me so much?" Claudia asked.

"I don't, dear. What I hate is the way you treated Charles."

"My marriage to him isn't any of your business."

"Except you made it my business when you trashed your apartment. I should have called the police on you that day."

Claudia rolled her eyes. "I'm leaving."

"Why?" Mrs. Wilson asked. "Are you afraid you'll be arrested for trespassing? I thought you had every right to be in your dead husband's apartment."

I arched an eyebrow at Mrs. Wilson. My dear

neighbor seemed to be egging on our intruder, but for what reason, I couldn't fathom. Was it out of sheer dislike, or was there more to it?

Mrs. Wilson smiled. "Tell me what you were looking for, Claudia, and I'll consider letting you walk out of here."

Sirens wailed in the distance.

"The will," Claudia said through gritted teeth. "I wanted to be certain any estate was coming to me instead of the stupid girlfriend."

"Ah, I see," Mrs. Wilson said, stepping aside and clearing the path for Claudia to run.

"Do you know where it is?" Claudia asked.

Mrs. Wilson shook her head. "I would never go through Charles' things. I have more respect for the dead than that."

Another cut. Dang. She was brutal.

"You disgust me," Claudia said. After throwing me a quick glare, she left.

"The feeling is mutual," Mrs. Wilson muttered under her breath.

We stood in silence for a few seconds as the sirens drew closer. "What do we do now?" I asked.

"You can go back to your apartment and I'll wait for the police if you like." She strode over to the kitchen table and picked up a few pages of

Charles' manuscript. "Such a shame. It looks as if he was writing a book."

"That's what I thought when I found the body. Maybe a memoir or something."

"Yes. One that will never be read." She ran her hand over the top of the typewriter.

"Sadly, no," I said. "I'm going to leave, but you were right about Claudia. She is a shrew."

Mrs. Wilson chuckled. "Yes. And it appears time has made her disposition even uglier."

Just as I closed the door to my apartment, I heard footsteps and men talking in the stairwell. Leaning my head against the door, I listened as Mrs. Wilson told the cops that Claudia had been caught in the apartment and she didn't know if the woman should be allowed in because she didn't live there. "It seems to be quite the gray area to me," Mrs. Wilson said. "I wasn't sure what to do."

I hobbled over to the telephone, picked up the business card Bill had given me and dialed the hotel number he'd written on the back.

"Bill Hart, please," I said to the friendly hotel front desk clerk.

"Mr. Hart has left the hotel, ma'am, and asked us to take messages from anyone who calls. Can I take your name and number for him?"

"Yes. Thank you." I gave my information then pulled the phone with me as I sat on the couch, hoping he wouldn't be too long. Not that I really had anywhere to go or anything to do.

I jumped when the phone shrilled through the silence. "Hello?"

"Hi, Patty. I received a note to call you."

Bill.

"I thought you may want to know that Mrs. Wilson and I just caught Charles' wife going through his things inside his apartment."

"What was she looking for? Did she say?"

"After a while, she admitted she was looking for his will."

"Interesting. Did she say anything else?"

"Not really," I replied, turning the cord around my finger as Ringo jumped onto the cushions and began rubbing his head against my arm. "She was angry she'd been caught though."

"Hmm... "

"I think she could have killed him, Bill. She hated him. I saw it in her eyes."

"I don't know, Patty. Women usually don't kill like that."

"But she has motive! If she's desperate enough

for the money, then she may have murdered him and come back looking for the will!"

A long stretch of silence sat between us while I ran my hand over my needy cat and it sounded like Bill was swirling ice cubes in a glass.

"I still think Wayne did it," he finally said. "That guy's guilty."

With a sigh, I rolled my eyes. "I think a jilted wife who obviously hates her husband makes for a better suspect than a man who lost his best friend."

"Are you arguing with an FBI agent, Patty?" Bill asked, chuckling.

"Yes. I guess I am. You seem to be focused on pinning this on Wayne, and I only hope you'll take others into account."

"I will," he replied. "I just can't see a woman killing a man like that. It kind of goes against the natural order of things."

"Fine, Bill. I'm sure you're right." I sighed in irritation at his unwillingness to really think about Claudia being the killer despite his agreement that he would.

"Listen, I was hoping you'd accompany me to see the war protestor who lives downstairs from you... the guy Charles used to fight with all the time."

"I don't know him."

"Really? I thought you did."

Again, I felt I was being used. "No, I don't."

"That's okay. Come with me anyway. I'd like to hear your thoughts on him after I complete the interview."

Well, maybe I wasn't being used. I had nothing to offer him except my company when it came to the man downstairs. "I suppose I could do that."

"Great. I'll be there tomorrow afternoon. Have a good night, Patty."

I hung up and scooped Ringo from cushion and returned the phone to the kitchen counter. Getting around without crutches wasn't so bad. Another day, and I'd be able to return to work.

After flipping on the television, I glanced over at the front door and noted I hadn't locked it.

I hurried over and turned the bolt as a chill ran down my spine. If I was right about Claudia and she had killed Charles, I certainly didn't need her coming after me for catching her snooping where she didn't belong.

Bill was wrong.

Of course, women had the fortitude to kill men by stabbing them, and I was determined to prove it to him.

Chapter 13

AT SOME POINT IN THE NIGHT, DONNA HAD returned. I found her snoring lightly, sprawled out on the couch, when I went to make coffee. Ringo lay on her chest, and I realized he was the reason I had been so cold during the night—he'd abandoned me for Donna.

I slipped on my green capris and a white button-down shirt. I debated wearing a hat since my hair refused to hang in its sleek bob but decided against it. No one at the library would care about my tresses.

"Where are you going?" she asked groggily as I pulled on my coat.

"To the library to do some research. Do you want to go with me?"

She sat up and nodded. "Not really, but I will. Can you give me a few minutes to get ready?"

"Sure. Hurry up, though. I want to be there right when it opens."

When Donna emerged from the bedroom looking chipper and dressed in a mini-skirt, boots, and a sweater, we headed out. I left my crutches at home, so we decided to grab the bus to avoid overextending my ankle.

People hustled about on the streets while the bus slowly meandered through traffic. I kept my eye on the women hurrying about, looking for new styles in clothing I needed to study. It seemed bell bottoms were becoming more and more popular and weren't just for hippies any longer. I appreciated the trend, but also loved my capris and wasn't sure I could give them up anytime soon.

Once we arrived at the library, we waited patiently for it to open.

"How was your trip?" I asked as Donna yawned.

"Fine. Uneventful."

"Did you see your pilot?"

Donna shook her head and sighed. I took that to mean she didn't want to discuss him, but something had happened between them. Maybe she'd dish the details later.

A few female college students joined us and I listened to them speak in serious tones about the book, *The Feminine Mystique* by Betty Friedan, one I had been meaning to read, but I hadn't gotten around to it. Donna stared off into the distance, obviously preoccupied by her own thoughts. I noted one of the girls didn't wear a bra and I tried to imagine the outright horror that would ensue if I arrived at work without one. Natural breasts wouldn't be tolerated. Everything had to be contained and as jiggle free as possible.

What would my life have been like if I'd had the opportunity to go to college? Perhaps I could have been a doctor or a lawyer, although both were typically a man's profession, and there was the problem that neither job really excited me. Would I have worn a bra? I certainly wouldn't bother with the awful girdle.

Perhaps I would have been discussing one of feminism's greatest books out on the city streets? Even if I had gone to college though, I'd still not know what to do with my life, so it was probably for the best I hadn't attended.

When the library opened, we allowed the

women to file in before us. I headed over to the card catalog and began my search.

"Do you ever feel inferior to them?" Donna asked.

"To whom?"

"To the college women. Do you believe they think they're better than us?"

I turned to my friend and shook my head. "No, I don't. Actually, I never gave it any thought. Why would you even consider such things?"

Although Donna was the life of the party, she often showed me little snippets of her psyche that indicated a very deep struggle with her self-esteem that I assumed went back to her less than stellar childhood.

Donna shrugged. "Sometimes when I hear them talking about books and math and such, I feel like they're better than me. I schlep drinks and pick up cigarette butts."

"You've also been to Paris," I said, laying my hand on her forearm. "You've traveled all over the country and seen things they never will. You know what to do to save lives if a plane goes down. They don't. No woman is more important than the other. We're all finding our own different paths."

Donna grinned and squeezed my hand. "You're right. I guess lack of sleep has me feeling down."

I'd always loved the library. The smell of books and the tranquility of it all often made me feel as if I'd stepped into another world.

"What are you looking for?" Donna asked.

"I'm researching women killers," I replied, digging through the cards.

Donna snorted and shook her head. "Heck, Patty. Nothing like a little light reading!"

"I know."

"Why in the world do you want to read about such horrible people?"

I didn't want to share that I was trying to prove an FBI agent wrong. Instead, I just shrugged and continued my task.

"I'm going to grab that table over there by the magazine rack," Donna said, pointing to empty seats by the window. "While you're doing your light reading, I'll dig into *Vogue*. I've been thinking I need a new look."

"Hmm… I don't know about that, Donna. You're stunning as you are."

"You're so sweet, Patty. But a girl can always freshen up her look. Like they say at work, we never know when we're going to meet our future husbands!"

I shook my head as she sauntered over to our spot. She was always thinking about marriage.

After fetching my books, I joined Donna at the table, which sat between the magazine rack and a bookcase. The sun shining through the window warmed the area nicely. In fact, I may have even had the urge to nap if it hadn't been for my reading material on women serial killers.

The depravity trapped on the pages astounded me. Jane Toppan, a nurse who went by the moniker "Jolly Jane" because of her upbeat temperament, had admitted to killing thirty-one people. Gesche Gottfried murdered fifteen people in fourteen years, including her parents, two husbands, her children and some friends. Nannie Doss murdered four husbands. The list went on, but one thing I noted was that all of them were killed with poison, not a knife.

Perhaps Bill had been correct. Maybe women didn't have the stomach to kill in such a bloody way. But the fairer sex certainly did have the fortitude to murder over and over, and the examples I'd studied proved that. Perhaps mental issues played a role.

Jane Toppan had been sentenced to a mental facility, deemed insane.

Of course, one could always look at Lizzie Borden, who had supposedly killed her parents with an axe. That must have been quite bloody. Had mental problems affected her?

Did Charles' wife, Claudia, qualify as crazy? Not from what I'd witnessed, but the woman who'd killed thirty-one people was also called Jolly Jane. On one hand, she was a happy and upbeat person, but on the other, she possessed a dark side where she enjoyed killing. People had many different sides to them. Claudia hadn't exactly been friendly and pleasant, but did she have that darkness within her?

Possibly. Perhaps she'd finally reached the top of her patience level with Charles about the divorce. Maybe Mrs. Wilson had been right and she'd killed for the money. She had motive, and I didn't think it was a smart idea to exclude her from the suspect list, no matter what Special Agent Bill Hart said about it.

"I think I need this green jacket," Donna said, bringing me out of my thoughts. "Wouldn't that look great with my eyes? With a little black eyeliner? It reminds me a bit of one Marilyn Monroe wore in that magazine."

The coat, a stylish number with large black buttons down the front and black lapels, would look nice with Donna's fair coloring. "I don't know, Donna. This is a pretty bold jacket. I think you'd need more than a little black eyeliner to really pull it off."

"Oh, I like that. Bold. I like being bold. Marilyn was bold in her own way, too."

Although Donna and I weren't friends when Marilyn had died, she'd shared many times how much she adored the actress.

"Look at Audrey Hepburn," she said, turning the magazine toward me. "Isn't she gorgeous? Her style is more subdued than Marilyn's but her beauty just jumps off the page. She's so sophisticated."

Large, soulful, intelligent brown eyes stared at me from the page. Her slight smile reminded me of someone harboring a secret she wanted to tell, but never would. Sophisticated and beautiful, indeed.

I smiled at my friend who didn't meet my gaze but she righted the magazine toward her and kept fingering through the pages. She seemed upset, and I had a feeling I knew why. "Are you sure you didn't see your captain?"

Donna sighed and slapped the magazine closed. "Fine. Yes, I saw him. He lied to me about his itinerary and I found him in a bar in Seattle making eyes at another stew while running his hand up and down her back."

"That's a bummer."

"He's a jerk." She picked up her magazine again. "I'm over him."

But she wasn't, and he'd hurt her terribly, no matter how much she tried to hide it. It became crystal clear the only reason she'd accompanied me to the library was so she'd have something else to concentrate on besides her wayward pilot.

I returned to my reading. After a few minutes, I shut the book, having had enough of female killers. "If you were going to kill someone, how would you do it?"

Donna glanced up at me, her brow furrowed. "Are you looking for advice or is this just a pretend scenario?"

"A pretend scenario. There's no one I really want to murder right now."

She finally smiled and folded her hands on top of the table. "It would depend on *why* I wanted to kill them."

"What do you mean?"

"What's my motive?"

"A customer who grabbed your bippy and gave

it a squeeze."

Donna threw her head back and laughed. "If he was cute enough, I may ask him if he wanted to marry, not kill him."

"You're crazy," I said, giggling.

"Now, if he was ugly, I think I'd slip a little something in his drink. Put him into an endless sleep while I pretended to have no idea of what happened."

Donna also defaulted to poisoning. How interesting.

"What about this scenario: You're married and your husband cheats on you? What do you do?"

She sat back and crossed her arms over her chest. "Well, if I was angry enough, I could see myself becoming physically violent. I wanted to hit the pilot when I found him at the bar."

"Do you think you could stab someone?"

Donna glanced out the window for a long moment. "In a fit of rage, possibly. It would depend on how angry and hurt I felt. I think I'd have to be out of my mind in order to put a knife in someone." She pulled out a silver flask from her purse and took a sip. "Do you want some?"

"No, thanks," I said, checking my watch. She'd

hit the bottle early, even by her own standards. "I have to get back soon. I'm meeting Bill."

"Who's Bill?"

"An FBI agent."

Donna's eyes widened. "I'm waiting for the punchline on this one."

"An FBI agent showed up to investigate Charles' murder. I guess you could say I've been helping him."

"Helping him how?"

Once again, I wasn't sure if I was actually assisting him or if he was using me, and if there was even a difference.

"He's asked me to go with him on some interviews."

"It sounds like he's making a move on you."

"I doubt it, Donna," I said with a shrug. "I think he's just trying to get his job done."

"Why is the FBI investigating a murder? Was Charles some government spy or something?"

I leaned forward after taking a quick glance around to make sure no one eavesdropped on us. "Bill is in charge of a serial killer task force," I whispered, aware that I was revealing Bill's secret when he specifically asked me not to. But Donna and I shared just about everything, so I knew she could be trusted. I harbored no guilt. "He was called in because he thought Charles may have been a victim."

Donna gasped and placed her hand over her mouth. "He was kind of a weirdo but... oh, my gosh. A serial killer!"

"Agent Hart says that he wasn't murdered by the serial killer though. So now, he's helping a friend in the police department by investigating the case."

Out of the corner of my eye, I noted the group of girls we'd waited with outside approaching us. I shook my head, hoping to indicate to Donna that the conversation had ended.

"Hey!" No-Bra Girl said. "We wanted to invite you to the rally this weekend." We each took the sheet of paper she handed us. "It's a women's equality march."

"We're also going to burn some foam domes!" her friend said. "We hope to see you there!"

As the girls found their next invite, I stared at the paper. I wouldn't burn any of my bras--they were too expensive and I needed them for work. However, I could probably be talked into tossing a girdle into the flames.

"Are you going to be around?" I asked Donna, holding up the piece of paper.

She shook her head. "I'm flying, but it would be fun to go."

"I think so, too," I murmured. "I'll be back to work by then, though. I hope so, anyway."

"Yes. We don't have that luxury. We've got to pay our bills."

I nodded and gathered my bag, then stood.

And solve a murder.

Chapter 14

INSTEAD OF COMING HOME WITH ME, DONNA mentioned a trip to the grocery store and a few other errands. We parted, and I met Bill back at my apartment where I shed my coat and purse. We then headed downstairs.

"What have you been up to today?" he asked as we rode the elevator.

"I went to the library to research women killers."

With an arched brow, he glanced over at me. "And how did that go?"

"It was interesting," I said, lacing my fingers together in front of me as I stared at the number above. "I do believe with the proper motive a woman can kill very easily... even with a knife."

"So, a crime of passion?" Bill asked.

"Well, I would say passionate rage. She'd have to be terribly angry. For instance, perhaps she's so furious her husband won't sign the divorce papers no matter how many times she asks."

"You really like Claudia for the crime, huh?"

The pieces fit: she had a motive. She had the ability to get close to Charles without him being worried or feeling attacked. Driving a knife into his stomach would have been easy if she had the guts to do it." Yet, something didn't sit quite right with me, although I couldn't pinpoint what. "I don't think she can be ignored just because she's a woman and I do believe her finances should be investigated. If she didn't kill him because he wouldn't sign the papers, perhaps she did because she's desperate for his money."

I couldn't meet Bill's gaze because I was afraid I'd find a look I had seen far too often in my life: a man staring at me with a condescending smile, almost as if he was sorry for how stupid I was.

"Well, I'll give it some consideration," Bill said. "It's a long shot, but she does have not one, but two possible motives. I doubt much will come of it, but I appreciate your efforts."

His response was better than I anticipated. I

pursed my lips together to hide my smile. A G-woman in the making.

"We'll need to make this interview quick," Bill said. "I have to catch my plane home."

A sinking feeling settled in my stomach when I realized I didn't want him to leave. He'd brought a new dimension into my life I never expected, and one that made me feel alive. Never could I have imagined that I'd be hanging out with an FBI agent and talking to potential murder suspects!

We reached apartment 2C and I could smell the weed being smoked inside even with the door closed.

"The super said this guy's name is Bob Briston," Bill said as he knocked.

My long-haired and heavily bearded twenty-something-year-old neighbor answered the door wearing nothing but a cloud of smoke. With a gasp, I averted my eyes from his thin frame.

In-the-Buff Bob.

"Mr. Briston?" Bill asked, waving his hand in front of his face to clear the haze.

"Come in, come in, man," Robert said, stepping to the side. "Even the fuzz can join us in our quest for peace and love."

Two things struck me as I stepped inside. First,

Bill hadn't even introduced himself and he'd been labeled a police officer. Was it the suit? The short hair? The closely shaven jaw? Second, Bob had company. I counted ten people lying on towels where the living room furniture should have been, all naked as the day they were born, chanting something indecipherable. The lights had been turned off, the windows covered in black paper, and dozens of candles lit the room. I coughed as the smell of marijuana, wax, and body odor all co-mingled in one overpowering scent.

"Oh, my word," I whispered as I tried to avoid seeing all the genitalia on display. No matter where I looked, I found more.

Bill held out his badge. "Are you Robert Briston?"

"That's my Christian name, but I go by Liberty, man. I'm truly free of all the trappings of this world."

Bill smiled and nodded. "Congratulations, Liberty. How lucky you are. I was wondering if we could talk somewhere private for a few minutes."

"Sure, man. Follow me."

The layout of the apartment was the same as mine. As he led us through the group of prone, chanting bodies into the bedroom, he bent over to pick up a lit joint. While I glanced away from that view, I recognized the people who lived on the other side of me—Dusk and Rainbow. They lay next to each other with their fingers intertwined, eyes closed. They seemed at peace, almost as if they were dead, but they contributed to the chanting. My stomach rolled and I tasted bile from the stench, so I covered my nose and mouth as we walked among the sea of bodies.

"It smells like you guys have been at the chanting for a while," Bill said, closing the door and flipping on the light. The room held two bare mattresses and a dresser. A shame none of the clothing hanging out of the open drawers was currently being used.

"Yeah, man. Two days of harmony and peace, of trying to find our true inner selves, of connecting with each other on the spiritual plane. It's been far-out, man. Enlightening, even."

"I bet," Bill muttered. "Way far out."

"What can I do for you, Mr. Po-lice?"

"I wanted to talk to you about the murder upstairs."

Liberty took a long drag from his marijuana joint, held it for a good thirty seconds, then tilted his chin back and slowly exhaled. "Do you want some?" he asked as he tried to hand me the cigarette.

"No, thank you," I said, unsure of what bothered me more: his nudity or the heavy fog settling in my head. Was I getting high for the first time in my life?

"You know, I could arrest you for that," Bill said, pointing at the joint.

"It wouldn't matter." He tapped his forefinger to his temple. "No matter where my body is, no matter what you do to me, I'm free up here. Man, no bars can cage me."

Would he feel that way while sober?

"What can you tell us about the murder upstairs?" Bill asked again.

"I don't know anything but love and peace, man. Nothing about the murder of the baby killer."

"That doesn't seem like a very lovable and peaceful thing to call someone," I said, crossing my arms over my chest. An image of Charles asleep on the couch with Ringo popped into my mind, and I bit my lip in anger. Charles had suffered greatly for his part in the war and hadn't needed to be reminded of it at every turn, which was exactly what In-the-Buff Bob continually did.

Liberty narrowed his gaze on me as he took another long drag. "Do I know you?"

"I lived next door to Charles," I replied. "He was my neighbor."

"Yeah, that's right. I've seen you around. You and that other fox hang out together." I assumed he meant Donna because almost everyone referred to her in that term, and they weren't wrong.

"For the final time, what can you tell us about Charles' death?" Bill asked, his voice agitated.

"Nothing. I know that guy went over to a land that doesn't belong to him to kill women and children for a war we shouldn't be in. I reminded him of it often to try to make him repent, but he never did. Dude used to freak out pretty hard."

"I'd be upset if someone continually called me such horrible names as well," I spat, realizing just how furious Liberty's actions towards Charles made me.

"Do you have a job, Mr. Briston?" Bill asked.

"I go by Liberty, remember? I'm not working for The Man. I'm free."

"If you don't work and sit around all day doing drugs, then how do you pay your rent?" I asked, fisting my hands at my sides. I'd completely forgotten about his nudity and now wanted to knock his teeth in. Was it my fury or the marijuana smoke that had made me so bold?

Liberty smoked and eyed me through the cloud.

"It's an excellent question," Bill said as he walked over to the window and opened it. I prayed for a gust of wind to air out the room. "How *do* you pay your rent, Liberty?"

"My parents believe in my quest for eternal harmony and peace."

"So your parents pay your way?" I asked, hoping I had deciphered that correctly.

"No. They believe in my quest."

"They pay his rent," Bill said, returning to my side. "I've seen it before. Kid comes from a wealthy family, becomes a hippy in search of love, peace and harmony, and the parents foot the bill for it all."

My head spun so badly from the drugs and the spoiled brat in front of me, I needed to sit down. "Must be nice not having to work to keep the lights on or buy your stupid drugs."

The man's smile faded and his brow creased for just a second. The easygoing fella was gone and I caught a flash of anger and hatred directed at me. Or had I? He quickly regained his composure. Maybe the drugs were making me see things that weren't there, or perhaps there was another side to In-the-Buff Bob——a dark killer.

"Is there anything else I can do for you?" he asked, his smile returning.

"Where were you that day?" Bill asked.

"Don't recall."

"I would suggest you try," Bill said. "Try really hard through that haze of smoke you have bathing your brain, Mr. Briston, or I may have to take you down to the station to sober up and remember."

Did he have the authority? I had absolutely no idea.

Just as Liberty brought the joint up to his lips again, Bill grabbed it and stubbed it out on the carpet. "Talk, you worthless stoner."

Liberty ground his jaw and stared at the burn mark. He probably wouldn't get his deposit back, but if his parents were financing, what did it matter? "Fine. I was downstairs in the streets fighting for my cause, for the good of all mankind."

The anti-war protest I'd been caught up in. Did he hear the contradiction of his words?

"*Fighting* for peace and love," Bill muttered with a chuckle, shaking his head. "Okay, Liberty."

"In fact, I was arrested."

Bill stared at him a moment, then pulled out his

paper pad and pen. In-the-Buff Bob had finally piqued his interest. "At what time?"

"In the afternoon, man."

"Do you know what time?"

"Man, time is like water to me. It just ebbs and flows infinitely through—"

"If you had to guess, put a number on it," Bill growled, losing his patience.

In-the-Buff Bob sighed, once again staring at the singed carpet. "Maybe three? Or five? I can't be sure."

"Thank you," Bill said. "We'll leave you to get back to your self-discovery."

As we walked back through the living room, I held my breath. Dusk and Rainbow were now sitting upright and passed a joint between them.

Rainbow jumped to her feet when our gazes met. With long blonde hair down to her waist, big blue sparkly eyes, and a never-ending smile that lit up a room, I'd always considered Rainbow the perfect moniker for her.

"Patty!" she exclaimed, taking me into a hug. "How have you been?"

I slowly wrapped my hands around her bare waist and tried not to cringe. With clothes on, the hug wouldn't have been so uncomfortable to me. "I'm good. It's lovely to see you as well."

Bill cleared his throat and I eased myself from her embrace. "We'll catch up sometime soon, okay?"

I trailed behind him and once we were out in the hallway, I inhaled deeply, thrilled to have fresh air in my lungs.

Bill checked his watch. "Listen, I'm going to head back to the police station and give them a report, then catch my flight out of here. Thanks for all your help during my stay."

His brusqueness surprised me. I'd thought we'd have time for a cup of coffee and discuss In-the-Buff Bob. "Do you think he did it?"

"It's possible," he replied with a shrug. "The timing works out. He could have killed Charles, gone down to the protest, and gotten himself arrested for an alibi."

"I was thinking the same thing."

"Well, they do say that great minds think alike," Bill said, then gave me a quick wink. "Give me a call if anything comes up, Patty... or if you want to chat. I'd like that."

"Good luck hunting your serial killer," I said as he walked away and waved over his shoulder.

I returned to my apartment while tossing around the case. In-the-Buff Bob had the opportunity, but upon finding Charles, I didn't remember any indication there'd been a scuffle of any kind. I couldn't see him allowing Bob into his home and to get close enough for the man to kill him.

Engrossed in my thoughts, I tried the door without thinking.

When I'd left Donna at the library, she'd mentioned a trip to the grocery store, so when my apartment door opened without me having to use the key, I stared at it for a long while. Maybe more time had passed than I'd realized and Donna had made it home before me.

"Donna?" I called as I entered and closed the door, my heart thundering, but she didn't answer.

I glanced around the apartment. Had I locked the door when I'd left with Bill? I tried to recall, but my mind drew a blank. The keys in my pocket dug into my hip, so I knew they were on me, but had I used them?

Goosebumps crawled over my flesh as fear gripped my chest. "Ringo?"

I moved into the kitchen and found a coffee cup on the counter, one that I was certain hadn't been there when I left. The couch cushions had been straightened and the blankets folded in a tidy stack. Had someone broken in to clean up, or was it some type of message?

"Ringo?" I yelled again.

A faint meow came from the bedroom, and I raced in there. The bedsheets were still in a crumpled mess and clothing lay strewn across the floor. Donna's suitcase hadn't been unpacked. However, the door to the bathroom had been closed.

I opened it and Ringo raced out.

Someone had locked him in.

Chapter 15

I PACED THE APARTMENT WAITING FOR DONNA TO arrive home. My first instinct had been to call the police, but I had to be certain she hadn't come back to the apartment, straightened up, then went to run her errands.

But why lock Ringo in the bathroom?

It wasn't anything she'd done before, and I prayed it was some type of mistake she'd made instead of facing the possibility that someone had been in our home. Perhaps Donna had used the restroom and closed the door, not realizing Ringo had been in there?

When the lock clicked, I hurried over and threw open the panel.

"Well, I'm glad to see you, too!" Donna said with a smile. "I was hoping you'd be home to help me. My arms are about to fall off from carrying all this stuff. This is definitely a man's work."

I grabbed a few of her parcels and she sighed in relief as I lugged them into the kitchen.

"There's a new clerk at the grocery store," Donna continued. "Cute as a button. Tall, thin, the dreamiest brown eyes… he asked for my phone number! I was excited at first, but I'm also on the rebound from the cheating pilot and I'm not sure I'm ready to—"

"Did you come home before you went shopping?"

Donna set down her bags and glared at me, obviously annoyed with my interruption. She must have also seen my apprehension because then her brow creased with worry. "What's going on?"

"Someone has been in our apartment," I said. "I came home and it had been tidied up a bit and Ringo had been locked in the bathroom."

Her eyes widened as she glanced around. "Are you sure? Was anything taken?"

"Not that I'm aware of."

"Who breaks into a place and cleans?"

"I... I don't know."

We stared at each other for a long moment, trying to come up with a logical explanation. I certainly couldn't think of one. When a knock sounded at the front door, we both jumped and Donna squealed, then cursed as she placed her hand over her chest.

Taking a deep breath, I tried to calm my racing heart before it beat out the front of my chest. "I'll get it."

I opened the door to find Beth, our fellow stew. She carried her overnight bag in one hand and a candy bar in the other.

"Hi, Patty!"

"Oh, my gosh... Beth! What are you doing here?"

"I'm on a layover and hoped I could crash here with you girls. So much more fun than hanging with the crew I was assigned. Ugh. What a bunch of downers!"

"Of course!" I said. "Come in. Donna! It's Beth!"

Donna hurried out from the kitchen. "Are you staying with us?" she asked as she embraced our friend.

"I hoped to!"

"We'd love to have you," Donna said, taking her bag. "Patty and I will take the bed and you can have our couch."

"It's very comfortable," I said, following the two into the living room. "I don't mind sleeping on it one bit."

As we chatted about where she'd flown in from, I twisted my hands in my lap while uneasiness continued to swirl around me. We'd just discovered our apartment had been violated and yet, we acted as if nothing had happened. I tuned them out as I glanced around the space, my stomach churning with worry. Who had been there? And why? Nothing seemed to be missing. Donna had left some gold earrings out on the dresser and they'd remained. Our coin jar still overflowed on the nightstand. We didn't have much of value, but none of it had been taken.

"Did you catch your killer yet, Patty?" Beth asked, bringing me back to the conversation.

"No, but she's hanging out with an FBI agent," Donna said.

Beth grinned and nodded. "Wow! How impressive. What does he have to say about all of it?"

"The case is still in the investigation stage," I said. "But I think he's got his sights set on Charles' friend, Wayne."

"What do you think?" Beth asked.

"There are a lot of other suspects who need to be looked into," I replied with a shrug. "I don't think Wayne did it."

"Someone broke into our apartment today," Donna blurted, and the mood between the three of us suddenly became heavier and more serious. Smiles faded and the air seemed to become thicker.

Beth arched an eyebrow, but then grinned and rubbed her hands together in excitement. "Really? Oh, gosh, I'm glad I decided to invite myself over. Tell me about it!"

When Donna had finished the tale, Beth's brow furrowed in confusion. "Are there any signs of someone forcing their way in?"

"No," I replied.

"So, did you lock the door when you left, Patty?" Beth asked.

I shook my head. "I can't remember."

"She's got a terrible memory," Donna said. "Can't remember names, especially."

"Okay, let's pretend that you *didn't* lock the

door," Beth said. "Who would come in here and straighten up?"

I met Donna's gaze and both of us shrugged.

"That's the part the doesn't make any sense," I said. "Nothing was taken."

"Very strange," Beth said. "However, I do wish someone would break into my apartment and clean."

Despite the heaviness of the conversation, the three of us giggled.

"If you *did* lock the door, who has a key?" Beth asked.

"Charles does… or did, I mean," Donna said. "I didn't give a key to anyone else. What about you, Patty?"

"No."

"Is it still in his apartment?" Beth asked.

"As far as I know," I said.

"Do you have a key to his place?"

"We do!" Donna said. "What are you thinking?"

"Let's go over and see if it's still there," Beth said. "At least we'll know if the key's been stolen. If not, you can grab it. If it has, you better talk to your super and get some new locks."

"Don't you think we should call the police?" I asked.

Beth shrugged, then stood. "It's up to you, but my guess is that all they're going to do is take a report. Nothing was stolen and whoever was in here cleaned up your apartment, which, as far as I know, is not a crime. It's just weird."

"They locked Ringo in the bathroom," I said when the cat jumped onto Donna's lap.

"I don't think anyone can go to jail for that," Beth replied. "What law was broken?"

She had a point.

"Come on," Beth urged. "Let's go check out Charles' apartment."

I grabbed Charles' key from the kitchen, and the three of us filed out into the hallway to find Mrs. Wilson leaving her place.

"Hello, girls!" she said. "What's going on in your exciting lives?"

I introduced her to Beth, then said, "Our apartment was broken into. Well, sort of."

"Oh, my word. Tell me what happened!"

Donna repeated the story, then said, "We're going to see if our key is still in Charles' apartment."

"What a good idea," Mrs. Wilson said. "I'll go

in with you, if you don't mind. Do you girls have a key?"

"Yes," I replied, holding it up.

"Okay, good. I was going to give you mine if you needed it."

We filed into the apartment. I had expected a blast of cold, stale air as I'd experienced before when I entered with Bill, but none came. Had someone recently been in there?

"Our key is right here," Donna said, pointing at the key rack hanging over the toaster oven in the kitchen. She held it up and I noted it had been labeled with a tag containing our names written in Charles' neat handwriting.

"Let's take that back," I replied.

"Can you? Would that be considered part of a crime scene or something?" Beth asked.

"No, it's no longer a crime scene," Mrs. Wilson said. "The police released it. There've been plenty of people rummaging around in here."

I recalled we'd found Claudia with a flashlight and she'd been very upset that we'd discovered her. "Have you seen someone else?" I asked.

"Karen was here earlier," Mrs. Wilson said.

"Did you speak to her?" Beth asked.

"Just a quick hello to see how she was."

"Do you think she would have broken into your place?" Beth asked.

"I don't see why," I replied. "I've never had any problem with her. Have you, Donna?"

She shook her head.

"I did mention to Karen that you were helping with the investigation," Mrs. Wilson said. "Also that the FBI had been here."

Beth and I exchanged glances. "If I'm remembering all the players correctly, Karen is the girlfriend, right?" she asked.

I nodded and had an idea of where her thought processes were leading. "Are you saying if Karen was the killer, and Mrs. Wilson told her that I was involved in the investigation, that she went into our apartment and... cleaned it?"

"She could be leaving some sort of message," Beth replied. "Just letting you know that she can get to you."

"Oh, my. That's a scary thought, but you could be right," Mrs. Wilson said.

Donna held up the key again. "Well, we have our key back, so she's not getting in again."

"Let's go pay Karen a visit," Beth said. "Have a little chat with her."

I realized she was completely caught up in the

moment and loving the drama and potential danger.

"You girls go about your business," Mrs. Wilson said. "I'm going downstairs to eavesdrop on everyone and talk with Mr. Killian for a bit."

As she hurried down the hallway then bound down the stairs, I turned back to Beth and Donna.

"I can only hope I have her energy when I'm her age," Donna said.

"She's impressive," Beth agreed. "But let's get back to Karen. Are we in agreement that we need to pay her a visit?"

"And say what?" Donna asked. "Ask her if she broke into our apartment?"

Beth shook her head. "No. Just ask about Charles, their relationship, and let her know that we know she was at his place. If she's not the one who broke in, she won't think anything of it. If she's guilty, then she'll realize we suspect her and take it as a warning."

"If she did kill Charles, I don't want to upset her and have her come after us with a knife," I said. "It could be dangerous."

"There are three of us," Beth said. "She's not going to try anything."

"Maybe not at that minute, but it's possible that

she could try something later," I countered. "Maybe we should call the police."

Beth narrowed her gaze on me and shook her head. "No. We aren't calling a bunch of men to swoop in and save the day. We are *women*, who are more than capable of handling ourselves against another woman."

"Well, I personally love it when a man swoops in," Donna said.

"Patty, we discussed this," Beth grumbled, ignoring Donna.

It was then I realized I had two polar opposite people standing in front of me. One who wanted nothing more than to be married and taken care of, and the other, an unapologetic feminist who wanted nothing to do with the traditional trappings of a woman's life. Then there was me, the one who wanted it all. Marriage and kids at some point in the future, and an important career now that didn't involve shlepping drinks and inhaling copious amounts of cigarette smoke.

"You're right," I said. "We'll go see her tomorrow."

"For now, let's break open a bottle of wine," Donna said. "It's happy hour somewhere, right?"

"Sounds like a great idea to me," Beth agreed.

Later that night, Beth snored softly on the couch while Donna and I dressed for bed.

"Do you think you'll be ready to head back to work soon, Patty?" she asked, slipping her nightgown over her head.

"I think so. My ankle is sore, but I can definitely get around on it."

Donna slipped into bed and fluffed up her pillow while I perched on the edge of the mattress and lathered lotion on my hands and arms. Ringo settled in between Donna's legs, purring loudly.

"I wonder what Karen's going to say tomorrow," Donna asked. "What do you think?"

"I have no idea, but it should be interesting, especially if she admits breaking into our apartment."

As I lay down on my own pillow, it made a strange crinkling sound.

"What's that?" Donna asked.

Rising from the bed, I pulled away the pillow to find a piece of paper neatly folded beneath it.

Both of us stared at it a moment, then Donna picked it up.

"What does it say?" I asked as she unfolded it.

She gasped, then she glanced up at me, her face

now pale and her gaze wide with fright. "Oh, my goodness," she whispered, handing it to me.

I took it and read the typed sentence. My hand began to tremble and I met Donna's gaze, then read it again.

Be careful. You don't want to get too close, or you could be next.

Chapter 16

THE NEXT MORNING, MY FEAR HAD WANED, BUT THE anger that had replaced it caused me to slam a couple cupboards, waking the other girls. Fine with me. Beth would be flying out in a few hours, and I wanted her to accompany Donna and me to meet Karen. After coffee, I slipped on my gray culottes, a pink sweater and my pink Mary Jane's. Donna opted for a multi-colored mini-dress and knee-high white boots, looking like she'd just stepped out of the pages of a fashion magazine. Beth wore a pair of jeans and a T-shirt.

"I want to make one quick stop before we go," I said, grabbing Charles' key.

"What for?" Donna asked.

"To check something in Charles' apartment."

We filed out of our own home and into his. At some point, someone would have to clean out the apartment and the super, Mr. Killian, would rent it out. Tears pricked my eyes at the thought of never seeing Charles again, but hopefully, someone as great would move in.

I hurried into the kitchen and sat down at the table. After gathering the stack of papers making up Charles' book into a neat pile, I looked over at the typewriter.

"Beth, can you please turn on that light?" I asked.

When the bulb above the table illuminated the space, I was able to study the ribbon. Looking at it from different angles, I thought I made out the imprint of a few letters, or was I only wishing?

Beth picked up the papers and began to rifle through them as I gently pulled on the typewriter ribbon to get a better look.

"You know, I think I just found his will," Beth muttered. "Well, his version of it."

"What does it say?" Donna asked.

"He says he wants everything to go to... oh, my gosh!"

"What?" Beth and I said in unison.

"He wanted all his things sold and the proceeds to go to his girlfriend, Karen."

"What's so surprising about that?" Donna asked.

"Well, he had a wife." Beth said.

"And he never signed the divorce papers," I said. "He never wanted his marriage to Claudia to end. It doesn't make any sense."

"But this whole thing is weird," Beth said. "He started writing a book, then switched to the will, then back to a book again."

"That is strange," Donna said. "It's like he lacked concentration or something."

"Yes."

I turned my attention back to the ribbon, threading a piece of paper into the machine and hit a few keys. As the letters appeared on the blank page, the ink disappeared from the ribbon.

"What are you doing, Patty?" Donna asked.

Ignoring her, I pulled the cartridge from the typewriter and brought it over to the kitchen sink where the light was brighter.

After gently pulling on the ribbon, I held it up to the sunlight and squinted. Yes, I could read what had been typed, and as the letters became words, and the words became sentences, I ground my jaw. The urge to throw the cartridge across the room overwhelmed me, but instead, I set it down on the counter and turned to my friends.

"Whoever typed that note to us did so on this typewriter," I said. "I can read the ribbon."

"What note?" Beth asked. "What am I missing?"

"Last night when we went to bed, we found a threatening note under the pillow," Donna said.

"It told us to be careful, not get too close, or we could be next," I said.

Beth's eyes widened. "And you can tell that it was written on that typewriter?"

I nodded and crossed my arms over my chest. "Karen had to be the one to type it. She was here. She had access to the apartment to get our keys. Perhaps Charles didn't write the will, but she did."

"You said Claudia was in here as well, though," Beth countered. "And what about his friend, Wayne? This apartment has been accessed by a lot of people."

"But the letter wasn't there until last night," I replied. "And why would any of them write a will that says Karen gets all his money? It doesn't make any sense."

"Maybe multiple people have used the type-writer," Donna offered. "Who is to say that only one person typed up the will and the letter?"

She had a point.

"Besides," Donna continued. "That letter could have been under the pillow for days. No one ever sleeps on that side of the bed, Patty."

Another valid argument. We both always slept on the left side of the mattress.

"Let's go talk to Karen and hear what she has to say," Beth said. "That letter is scary, but we don't know who wrote it or when they placed it under the pillow."

DONNA HAD RECALLED Karen mentioning she had an apartment a few miles away in the Sunset District and we were able to verify the exact address in Charles' address book. We debated whether to tell her we were coming but decided against it. Regardless of whether she was involved in Charles' murder or not, she wouldn't appreciate the intru-sion. I certainly wouldn't if I was in her shoes.

After the cab ride, we stood in front of the building. My stomach flip-flopped and suddenly my initial anger at the letter fled. In its place, I had a case of the nervous jitters. Confronting a potential murderer with my friends seemed far more dangerous than meeting one with an FBI agent.

"We shouldn't approach her like this," I said. "I don't want to accuse her of something she didn't do. If she did kill Charles, she'll feel threatened."

"I agree," Donna said.

Beth rolled her eyes. "Would you two stop? We're just going to have a little chat with her, not accuse her of writing the letter or murdering her boyfriend."

"Don't forget she could have typed up that will and left it for someone to find," I said, glancing up at the unattractive building that had seen better days. "I hate to say it, but this looks like a horrible place to live."

"Maybe they just haven't kept up the outside," Donna said, chewing her nail. "The inside could be really nice."

Beth and I exchanged glances, and I could see she doubted the statement as well. "Let's go in," I said with a sigh.

I'd been correct—the owners of the apartments hadn't taken care of any area of the building.

Cracked, greenish linoleum greeted us in the lobby. Graffiti covered one of the gray walls.

"This place should be condemned," Donna whispered. "Can you imagine being a woman living alone here? My word, I'd be terrified!"

The elevator had a ripped and yellowing *out of order* sign hanging from it, indicating it hadn't worked in quite a long time. Thankfully, Karen lived on the first floor. My ankle wasn't having any issues when I walked, but I didn't want to discover if the stairs would set my healing process back. My armpits still ached from the stupid crutches.

Beth knocked on Karen's door.

"Who is it?" she called from the other side.

"I wouldn't answer my door if I lived here, either," Donna whispered.

"It's Charles' neighbors," I called. "Donna and Patty. Remember us?"

The door slowly opened and the petite woman with mousy brown hair and eyes stared at us with uncertainty. "What are you doing here?"

"I'm Beth. It's lovely to meet you Karen," she said as she pushed past the woman without an invitation.

Donna and I filed in. I gave Karen a weak smile

which I hope conveyed I was truly sorry for the intrusion.

"We came to talk to you about Charles," I said as she closed the door. "I hope that's okay."

"I... I guess so."

"Can we sit?" Beth asked.

Karen nodded and Donna wrapped her arm around her shoulders. "I'm really sorry about your loss, hon. Charles was a good fellow."

"Thanks. Why are you here?"

Sitting on the pea-green sofa, I glanced around the studio apartment. The walls had been painted an eye-searing sunshine yellow, and I realized Karen didn't have a window to bring in any natural light. The unmade bed sat a few feet to my right with a table and lamp acting as illumination for both areas. Directly across from me stood the kitchen sink and short refrigerator, as well as a clothing rod that held hangers filled with dresses and pants. Her shoes were neatly lined up directly underneath. I assumed the curtain to the left of the sink led to the restroom area. And I had thought the apartment I shared with Donna was tiny. Overall, I found the place quite depressing and it became apparent Karen definitely had motive. If her living conditions were any indication, she was barely getting by.

"As I mentioned, we wanted to talk to you about Charles," Beth said. "Have the police been around asking you about his death?"

"No. They called and said they would stop by, but they never did."

My head snapped to her attention. "The police never came?"

Karen shrugged. "Not that I have much to add to the investigation. Charles was here one day and gone the next."

"Were you two in love?" Donna asked.

"I thought we were," Karen said. "But then I found the divorce papers he never signed last week while I was straightening up his place. They had fallen behind the dresser."

"How did that make you feel?" I asked. "It must have been hard knowing your boyfriend was someone else's husband."

"Oh, I was furious," Karen said. "Raging mad. I felt betrayed and used."

"Did he give you an explanation as to why he never divorced his wife?" I asked.

"He said that he'd forgotten about it," she replied, shrugging.

"Forgotten about his divorce?" Donna asked incredulously. "That's ridiculous. No one forgets about a divorce."

I had to disagree with Donna. Marriage may be at the forefront of her mind at all times, but it wasn't that way with everyone. Charles might have put his split with Claudia behind him and forgotten about the unsigned papers, especially if he was more focused on his mental state, or high from smoking his marijuana.

"Did you believe him?" Beth asked.

Karen sighed and rubbed her temples for a moment before speaking. "I loved Charles very much," she said. "I can't tell you if I truly believed him or if I *wanted* to believe him. Do you know what I mean?"

Donna nodded and reached over to grab Karen's hand. "I do. Sometimes we want things to be true, so we overlook what's directly in front of us that would force us to see the lie we're living."

I stared at my friend, surprised by her honesty. She spoke from the heart, from her own knowledge and mistakes.

"That's exactly right," Karen said. "I couldn't have said it better myself.

"How did you two meet?" Donna asked. "Was it a random thing, or something really romantic?"

Karen's eyes welled once again as she shrugged. "We met at the grocery store, if you can believe that. We were both looking at the lettuce. He asked me the best way to tell if the lettuce was fresh, or if it had been around for a while. The conversation came easy, and the next thing I knew, I was saying yes to a dinner date."

"That's definitely romantic," Donna said, sighing. "That's why I'm always on the lookout for my husband. I could meet him on the plane, or in the produce section. We just don't know when we're going to find the one for us, do we?"

Glancing over at Beth, I noticed her gaze had narrowed and doubt shone from her eyes. She wasn't buying Karen's and Donna's epiphany, and frankly, I wasn't either. What was so romantic about lettuce?

Beth cleared her throat. "I find it odd the police haven't been here."

Frankly, I did as well. Why hadn't they bothered to interview the girlfriend? She had as much motive as Claudia, and glancing around her sad apartment, perhaps even more so. Was it because they were so focused on the killer being a man?

Yes, Karen was small in stature and quiet in demeanor, but that didn't mean she couldn't kill, especially in a fit of rage. She'd fully admitted finding the divorce papers had greatly upset her.

"I don't have an answer to you on why they've never come, but I do need to get to work," she said. "I wish you would've called."

"Where do you work?" Beth asked.

"I'm a waitress at the burger joint up the street."

"Oh! Is that the place with the cute pink uniforms?" Donna asked.

"Yes. Exactly."

"Isn't that also the place where the waitresses aren't paid as much as the waiters?" Beth asked.

"Unfortunately, yes," Karen said. "There's been quite a few protests in front the restaurant about it. A lot of the college girls come over and march."

Beth rose to her feet. "Good for them. Women should be earning the same as men for the same work. It makes me furious that this is even an issue in today's society. We're still stuck in the forties and fifties."

"A raise would definitely be nice," Karen said. "So would a little time off to mourn Charles, but my boss already told me that isn't going to happen."

Beth swore under her breath and shook her head. "Miserable, wretched men."

"Not all men are horrible," Donna said.

"Her boss is," I replied. "Karen should be allowed to grieve."

"I really need to go," Karen said. "I'm going to be late."

We said our goodbyes and left the sad building. The three of us didn't speak until we were back inside our apartment.

"So, what do you think?" Donna asked, stretching out on the couch like a lazy cat caught in a ray of sunshine.

"I think she's a great possibility," Beth said. "The more I think about it, the more I'm convinced a woman did this."

"Why?" I asked, pushing Donna's legs off the sofa so I could sit down.

"It just seems that's what makes sense to me," Beth said. "You've got the wife and the girlfriend."

"There's also Wayne, the friend he owed money to," I said. "And don't forget the guy downstairs... Liberty."

"I never got the chance to ask you how that went," Donna said. "What happened?"

"Not a lot," I replied. "They were having some

sort of... I don't even know what to call it. A hippy fest? Anyway, everyone was high and naked and Liberty said they were meeting each other on a spiritual plane or something like that."

"Do you think he could have killed Charles?" Donna asked.

I thought about the conversation and nodded. "He didn't show any remorse. I think in his mind, Charles being dead is a good thing."

Beth glanced at the clock, then cursed. After grabbing her uniform, she hurried into the bedroom, emerging soon after dressed for work. "I'll see you girls later," she said. "Thanks for the wine and excitement. You'll have to keep me posted on what happens!"

Donna and I walked her to the door and said our goodbyes. I made sure to lock up behind her.

"She sure doesn't like men," Donna said, shaking her head. Then, she lowered her voice. "Do you think she may be queer?"

Her question caught me off guard. I'd never met a person who I knew for a fact was gay. "I... I have no idea."

"Not that it matters. I was just wondering," Donna said. "More importantly, do you think we're safe here? I actually felt better with Beth around."

"I know. I did as well. I think we're okay, though."

Donna sighed, turned on the television, and sat down on the couch. "I never thought I'd say it, but I can't wait to go back to work. Knowing someone's been in our apartment and wondering who killed Charles gives me the creeps."

I couldn't have agreed more.

Chapter 17

Our phone rang before daylight. I'd moved it to the kitchen last night so I wouldn't trip over the cord. I staggered over to it to answer as I heard Donna moaning from the bedroom. That bottle of wine she'd consumed the previous evening must not have agreed with her.

"Hello?"

"Patty?"

"Yes?" I said, my voice cracking.

"It's Linda Delaware." For a second, I couldn't place the name in my sleep-induced haze, but then I realized I was speaking to my work superior, one of the stewardess managers. I immediately stood up straight, threw back my shoulders, and sucked in my stomach, just as I would have during an inspection. "Hi, Linda. What can I do for you?"

"You and Donna need to come in immediately," she said. "I have a flight to New York today and I don't have a crew. Five girls live together and they all came down with the flu. Why you girls insist on shacking up like that, I'll never understand."

"We don't make enough money to live on our own," I said, quickly wishing I could take it back. Shutting my eyes, I twisted the phone cord around my finger while mentally berating myself. Complaining to a superior probably wasn't a smart thing to do.

"The flight leaves at eight," Linda said crisply. "Please hurry in."

Donna staggered from the bedroom. "What was that about?"

"Well, I've got good news and I've got bad news," I said, placing the phone on its cradle.

"It's too early for either," she mumbled.

"The bad news is that we've been called in. A bunch of girls who live together have the flu."

"What's the good news?" she asked, rubbing her temples with the tips of her fingers.

"We're going to New York."

She stilled for a moment, then met my gaze with a grin. "New York?"

"Yes."

"Well, put the coffee on, Patty! Let's get going!"

My excitement at seeing New York again over-rode any irritation I had at the early morning phone call. I'd been to the fabulous city once, and I couldn't wait to go back. There was so much to see, so much to do.

"Hopefully, the weather will hold up for us!" Donna said as she packed her overnight bag. "What should we do when we get there? Times Square? Broadway? Oh, my gosh. Do you think we can get a reservation at Delmonico's? Maybe if we look foxy enough, we could get into Copacabana!"

"Well, if we're shooting for Copacabana, I better wear something of yours. I don't own anything overly sexy!"

As we discussed other potential plans and packed, my excitement grew. Finally, I'd be out of the apartment and able to forget about the murder, even if just for a little while.

Ringo stalked into the bedroom and curled up on the mattress. His head moved from me to Donna while we talked and after a few minutes, he meowed loudly.

We both stopped folding our clothing and looked at him. Guilt washed through me when I realized he'd be left alone.

"Oh, Ringo," Donna said with a sigh as she tossed her nightgown into the overnight bag. "I'm sorry, buddy." She picked up the tabby and gave him a quick snuggle. "You're going to have to stay home by yourself."

I quickly zipped my bag and hurried over to Donna, then kissed the tip of Ringo's nose. "We need to get going," I said softly. "Please, please don't tear anything apart."

"Or pee on anything," Donna added.

We picked up our bags and walked to the door, then exchanged glances. Both of us knew we'd arrive home to something destroyed or soiled. The cat hated being left alone.

"Let's ask Mrs. Wilson to watch him," Donna suggested.

"I feel awful waking her at this time of the morning. The sun isn't even up."

"We can slip a note under her door along with the key. She just needs to check in on him for a few minutes."

"Okay. That sounds like a good idea."

Donna ran back inside and emerged a few

minutes later, then placed the note and key under Mrs. Wilson's door.

We took the elevator downstairs to our waiting cab. Once we were situated in the backseat and on the way to the airport, Donna leaned over and whispered, "I decided to try and get away with not wearing a girdle."

I burst out laughing, but secretly wished I was brave enough to do the same.

When we arrived at the airport, I pulled out my compact and did a quick touch up before entering. Smiling, we walked through the sea of people eyeing us. I waved at a couple of kids while Donna greeted a few businessmen, always on the lookout for a husband.

We fell in line for our inspections.

"Donna, I hope you have your girdle with you," Linda said. "I saw your hips jiggling when you walked in."

I snickered as Donna rolled her eyes. "Yes, I do. It was an oversight, Linda. I'll go put it on right now."

"Thank you, dear. And Patty... where are your heels?"

I'd worn my most comfortable shoes—a navy blue pair of Mary Janes that matched my uniform.

"If you recall, I sprained my ankle last week," I replied. "I didn't think I'd make it through the day in my heels."

"Ah, yes. I forgot about that. Very well, but we need you back in your heels as soon as possible. The Mary Janes give you a clunky look instead of the long, sleek profile we prefer our stews to have. You do look pleasantly refreshed, Patty. Well done on getting your rest."

I smiled, delighted that Linda was happy with me.

"However, you do need some lip coloring. Please add a little something, okay?"

I reached for my bag and pulled out my Mary Quant lipstick—a very light shade of pink that really made my blue eyes stand out.

When inspections were finished, Linda approached me once again. "Patty, for this flight, you'll be at the front of the plane. Donna will be stationed at the back. Your head stew will be Marsha. Have you two ever met?"

"I don't believe so," I replied, trying to keep the excitement out of my voice. The front of the plane! Wow! Donna may have had her trip to Paris, but I was finally moving up!

Linda called Marsha over and introduced us. A

bubbly woman with brown hair, green eyes, and a bright smile took my hand in hers and seemed incredibly excited to meet me. "We're going to have an excellent flight! I can feel it in the air!"

I grinned at the thick Texas accent, which immediately brought Special Agent Bill Hart to mind.

Had he caught his serial killer yet?

Donna, Marsha, and I crossed the tarmac and climbed up the stairs to our awaiting plane. Once we had our bags tucked away, we began our examination of the interior, making sure all was right for our onboarding customers.

When the pilots arrived, we greeted them and everyone introduced themselves, then they moved to the cockpit. I had previously only met the co-pilot, a nice man who, based on his sheer physical size, should have been a football player. I'd dubbed him Large Larry.

"The customers are coming!" Marsha called, and I hurried up to my spot at the front of the plane, leaving Donna at the back. I smiled, threw my shoulders back, sucked in my stomach, and took my place next to Marsha.

"You sounded like Paul Revere there," I whispered, keeping my gaze on the line of people crossing the tarmac.

She laughed and grabbed my hand. "I can tell flying with y'all is going to be great fun!"

As the customers filed up the staircase, we welcomed them, checked their tickets, and pointed them to their seats. We raced to help people with bags, hang coats, and retrieve coffee and cocktails. Before I knew it, the time had come for takeoff.

With a sigh, I took my jump seat next to Marsha and closed my eyes for a few moments. It would be the only time I had to rest before we began service for the coast-to-coast flight. A child began crying a few rows back, and I made a mental note to grab some crayons to placate her, as well as to see about a trip to the cockpit. I'd never flown with our captain and co-pilot, so I hoped they'd be open to seeing children. I loved watching their faces light up when they entered the important space and received their airline pin.

The loud rumbling of the plane made a cat-nap impossible, but when we were given the all-clear to begin breakfast preparation, I took two aspirin for my ankle that had begun to act up, and I was ready.

Breakfast consisted of cheese omelets, a danish and a fruit bowl, and of course, a white rose. The coffee and tea flowed, as did the grapefruit juice and mimosas. I handed out magazines, crayons for the children, and chatted with a few women about my life as a glamorous stew—then fetched a cigarette butt from the floor. Glamorous? In the advertisements, yes. But when it came down to the nuts and bolts of reality, the actual job couldn't be described as such. Why people couldn't deposit the garbage in the ashtrays, I'd never understand.

"Any more coffee for you, sir?" I asked a man who resembled Bob Crane so closely, I almost asked if he was the actor.

"No, thank you," he replied pleasantly with a smile.

I returned to the front galley where I found Marsha preparing a tray. "That guy in 4C resembles Bob Crane."

She glanced over at me and smiled. "It *is* Bob Crane, silly."

I gasped and glanced around the corner at him again. "Are you sure?"

"Yes. He's very dreamy, isn't he? I've had him on my flight a few times."

"I have to tell Donna," I said. "She loves him."

"Sure. Just make sure she doesn't fawn over him too much. He doesn't like the attention, and we want to keep him coming back to our airline, not send him somewhere else."

Could Donna meet one of her favorite actors without become a star-struck blabbering idiot?

I was about to find out.

After delivering my drinks, I hurried down the smoke-filled aisle to Donna and whispered my findings.

Her eyes widened and she almost dropped her tray. "Are you kidding me? Don't mess with me on this one, Patty. Bob Crane is *here*? On *this* plane?"

"No, I'm not kidding you, but you need to play it cool. He's in 4C. Go say hello and get your autograph." I took her tray. "I'll deliver these, but hurry back."

Thankfully, Donna had a napkin under each drink with its assigned seat written on it. While handing out the glasses, I kept my eye on her. She smiled and chatted quietly while Mr. Crane signed the piece of paper she'd handed him. When she returned to her station, she beamed with happiness.

"You can kill me now," she said with a sigh. "I've met Bob Crane. He's just so nifty. Thanks, Patty."

I grinned and squeezed her arm. "You're welcome."

"This trip couldn't get any better. I mean, we're on our way to New York with Bob Crane on the plane! Oh, my word. What's next? We meet the Beatles?"

The flight went on smoothly. No one got overtly drunk, the kids played quietly after getting to see the cockpit and meet the captains, and the stews performed like a well-oiled machine. Not even a moment of turbulence disturbed us. It was one of the easiest flights I'd had since getting my wings, despite the length. Even my ankle behaved and didn't cause me too much trouble.

When we landed, we said our goodbyes to the passengers, then retrieved our own things. We headed inside the airport, where I caught a glimpse of a pretty blonde stew wearing our airline uniform carrying a sign with my name on it.

"Look at that!" Donna said, pointing at the woman. "Patty, what's going on?"

"I… I don't know," I said, now concerned something had happened to my family. They didn't like my job and our relationship had become terribly strained, but that didn't mean I didn't care or love them. If one of them had become sick… or worse, I'd be devastated.

I weaved my way through the crowd.

"I'm Patricia Byrne," I said once I stood before the woman. "What's happened?"

"You've received an urgent call," she said, handing me a piece of paper. "From the FBI."

I opened the folded note and read Bill's name and number.

"He said it's imperative that you phone him as soon as you get to your hotel," the stew continued. "He wants you to call collect. It's urgent."

Donna stared at me as my good mood slowly deflated.

"I hope you aren't in trouble," the stew said, her New Jersey accent thicker than sludge. "The flu's going around and our airline can't afford to have too many other stews out."

"Don't worry," Donna said. "She hasn't done anything wrong. We'll be here tomorrow to catch our flight."

She smiled. "Excellent. Have a fun time in New York!"

Had something happened with Charles' murder? That had to be it. Why else would Special Agent Bill Hart track me down in New York?

Chapter 18

WHEN WE ARRIVED AT THE HOTEL, WE QUICKLY checked in and I headed to my room, relieved the airline had given us each our own space. I wanted privacy while I spoke to Bill.

I kicked off my shoes and pulled off my uniform and girdle, leaving them in a pile on the carpet. Taking a moment, I stood with my eyes closed, appreciating the freedom as the cool air caressed my skin before sitting down on the bed in my bra and underwear. I suddenly had a good case of the nerves and the urge to reach for a cigarette, but I didn't have any. Instead, I grabbed the pen next to the phone and held it in my hand as I would if I were smoking. Then, I dialed to request an outside operator.

"I'd like to place a collect call, please."

"Of course," the friendly woman said. "Do you have the number, or shall I look it up for you?"

"Yes, I have it." I read off the digits Bill had given me. It rang three times before he answered and I realized he'd given me his direct line.

"Bill Hart," he growled. Someone was having an off day.

"This is the operator, sir. I have a collect call from Patricia Byrne. Do you accept the charges?"

"Yes, ma'am," he replied, his voice suddenly far perkier. "Thank you."

When the operator clicked off, Bill and I both started talking at the same time. We laughed and he said, "You go first."

"What's going on, Bill? Why did you call the airline and have me tracked down?"

"Honestly?"

"Of course!" I replied with a huff. "I didn't rush to the hotel to call you to listen to lies!"

"I wanted to hear your voice, Patty."

A slow blush crept up my neck to my cheeks. I flopped back on the mattress with a sigh as relief swept through me.

"I've been trying to call your apartment all day, but there wasn't an answer. So, I phoned the airline and confirmed you were working. As soon as they learned I was with the FBI, they quickly agreed to look up your flight and get a note to you."

"That's really sweet, but I wish you wouldn't have told them it was urgent. You scared me."

"I'm sorry about that," he replied, chuckling. "Like I said, I wanted to hear your voice, not wait around until you had a chance to phone. My call, me tracking you down, the message... it was all purely selfish. I figured with you being in New York, you'd choose dinner in Time Square over a chat with me."

"Well, don't do that again," I scolded, shaking my head. "Unless it truly is urgent, of course."

"My apologies, ma'am."

I wasn't pleased with Bill's actions, but I did appreciate him wanting to speak with me. My relationship with him both excited and confused me. Sure, I had offered to help him in the investigation of Charles' death, but then sometimes he was so gruff with me, I felt he was taking advantage. But then he'd used his power to track me down through the airline and have me phone him. Not exactly the actions of someone using another. "How's your serial killer case going?' I asked.

"Not good," he said, sighing. "It's really frustrating. But we'll get him eventually."

I thought back to my research on women killers. All those who had murdered multiple people had eventually been caught. I could only hope the same would happen for Bill.

But how many murderers walked the streets without being apprehended? Hundreds? Maybe thousands?

"What about you?" he asked. "Has Charles' murder been solved yet?"

"Not to my knowledge," I said. "If it has, I haven't received word of it. I would think you'd know more than me with your connection to Detective Peterson."

"Are you still nervous about living there?"

"Most definitely," I replied, twirling a piece of hair around my finger as I stared at the popcorn ceiling, the little bubbles forming pretend pictures in my mind's eye. "I think I will be until the killer is caught."

"Do you have any other leads?"

"Well, we went to visit Karen, Charles' girlfriend. Did you know the police never interviewed her?"

"No. I haven't talked to Detective Peterson since I left."

"Why wouldn't they interview his girlfriend, Bill? It doesn't make any sense to me."

"Maybe it was an oversight, or maybe they've found a lot of evidence on Wayne and they're closing in."

"Hmm... I still don't think Wayne did it."

"I don't know what to tell you, Patty. The police follow the evidence and if it's leading them to Wayne... well, he's their man. The killer would need motive and opportunity. Wayne had both. Charles owed him money, and I found someone who placed him at the apartment building earlier in the day."

Well, what a surprise. "I didn't know that," I said. "Why didn't you tell me? Who is it?"

"I'm telling you now. And sorry, but I can't let a stew in on every aspect of the investigation."

But he could sure use me to get introductions to everyone he suspected. I had been dealt the short end of the stick on the information aspect of the case.

With a sigh, I sat up and studied the room. I hadn't noticed it when I first entered because I had been so focused on calling Mr. Coffee. The dark wood paneling gleamed with the sun streaming through the opening in thick, floor-length blue curtains. Running my hand over the yellow comforter, I was surprised by its softness and wondered if it was new. The opposing wall matched the bedspread, and held a dresser, the television sitting on top. Overall, I found the space clean and comforting.

"If they arrest Wayne, I think they've messed up their jobs," I replied. "He's not the killer. I know it in my gut."

"You sound pretty sure of yourself," Bill replied with a chuckle. "Especially for someone who has no training or experience with murder investigations."

I knew he hadn't wanted to be condescending— he only spoke the truth. I didn't have any training or expertise, but I did know how to read people, and that counted for something. Unless, of course, Wayne was some type of psychopath who was able to hide his true self. From what I'd witnessed, he had been the most honest out of everyone I'd talked to about Charles' death.

But evidence and facts would decide, not my hunches.

"Next time you're in Dallas, will you give me a call?" Bill asked. "I'd love to see you again. We could have lunch or dinner... whatever your schedule permits."

I smiled as my heart pattered, but I didn't want to sound too eager. Frankly, I was irritated he'd held back information on the case from me, even though I shouldn't be. As he liked to remind me, I was only a stew, not an officer of the law. "I'm not sure when my next flight there will be, but I'll let you know."

"Please do," Bill said. "And have a great time in New York. Do you fly out tomorrow?"

"Yes."

"Okay. Have fun but be careful."

"Yes, sir, Mr. FBI. I won't go home with any strangers."

"Good girl. I hope to talk to you soon. Keep my number and call me anytime."

With a grin, I placed the receiver on the cradle and stared out the window for a few moments. I was actually quite tired, but New York awaited me, so I'd have to find the energy to do the town. Besides, Donna would never forgive me if I stayed in.

A knock sounded at my door. Speaking of Donna...

"Are you ready to go?" she called.

"Not quite," I said, hurrying over. I opened the

panel, keeping myself hidden behind it in hopes of avoiding being the lingerie show for anyone walking by in the hallway.

Donna swooped in wearing a tan suede mini-skirt, matching boots, and a black turtleneck. She came bearing clothes and a white pair of low-heeled go-go boots. Her blonde bob had been coiffed to perfection, and her black eyeliner was on point, highlighting her blue eyes. Pale pink lipstick covered her lips. "Patty, you're standing here in your underwear. We're supposed to be leaving! We have exactly fifteen hours left in New York and we're wasting precious minutes. What are you going to wear?"

"I was thinking about my blue dress."

"Ugh," she replied, rolling her eyes. "No way. You'll look like a throwback from the fifties." She tossed the clothing at me. "Put this on."

I slipped on the hot pink, long-sleeved dress that fell to my mid-thigh.

"And wear these," Donna said. "They shouldn't hurt your ankle, but you'll still look foxy as heck."

I sat on the bed and slipped on the boots.

"You haven't even done your makeup, Patty," Donna said, shaking her head, obviously exasperated with me. "Do a quick touchup and let's blow this pop stand."

I quickly ran into the bathroom and combed my hair, added a little lipstick and eyeliner, then did a quick check in the mirror while I ran my hand down the front of the dress. Of course, Donna had been right. The pink dress looked fantastic with my black hair.

"Are you ready?" she called.

"I am." I emerged with my hands on my waist and slowly spun around while tossing my hair as if I were a model.

"Yes, you are!" Donna squealed, rising from the bed. "Let's go have some fun!"

"Did you call your FBI agent?" She asked as we rode the elevator down.

"Yes."

"What did he want? Is everything okay?"

The door opened and a couple stepped in, smiled, then turned their backs to us.

"Everything's fine," I whispered. "He said he just wanted to hear my voice."

Donna smiled. "He's sweet on you, Patty."

"We'll see about that," I said with a shrug. "He can be nice one moment, then almost condescending the next."

"Typical man," Donna said, shaking her head.

The couple in front of us glanced over their shoulders. The woman's lips curved knowingly, while the man furrowed his brow and glared. Donna and I gave them our best, friendliest stewardess grin. When the elevator came to a stop, they stepped out.

"They need to mind their own business," Donna said.

"I agree." We met Marsha in the lobby and the three of us strode out the hotel onto the bustling streets of New York.

After walking across Time Square, we grabbed dinner and drinks at an Italian joint where the garlic bread was so strong, it probably put a little curl in my hair. We took a cab to the Copacabana, but the line stretched for blocks to get in, so we opted to return to the hotel where we found the bar with a live jazz band playing and a group of businessmen offering to buy us drinks.

After hours of flirting, dancing and laughing, the bar closed. I helped Donna to her room, then stumbled to my own. Thankfully, we'd been placed on the same floor. I did manage to remove my boots before crawling into bed, but I didn't wash my face or take off the dress. Hopefully, my complexion would remain clear for our pre-flight inspection. My ankle throbbed but I tried to ignore it. I'd over-done it on the dance floor with a cute ad manager from one of the city's firms. Cut-a-Rug Karl, I'd dubbed him, who'd also asked for my number. I declined to give it to him. He had been nice enough, but I didn't need long distance phone calls raising my phone bill, and I certainly wasn't the type of girl with a man in every port, so to speak. I'd leave that to other girls who liked juggling their men. Still, I'd been flattered he'd found me inter-esting enough to ask.

As I lay in bed, the city that never sleeps was still alive. The hum of traffic filtered up to my room providing a nice, lulling sound that relaxed me.

Or it could have been all the gin and tonic I'd consumed.

No matter how much fun I'd had, I still couldn't stop thinking about Charles' murder. It seemed to be like a mosquito bite that wouldn't quit itching. Just when I could fully concentrate on what Cut-a-Rug Karl had to say, a little voice reminded me Charles' killer was still at large and no one knew who it could be. Just like a mosquito bite, that little voice drove me nuts. I couldn't help but feel that my subconscious mind knew who the killer was, but it wasn't ready to reveal it to me quite yet.

And that scared me. If I was right, I'd come face-to-face with a murderer. I'd spoken to them, possibly shook the hand that had plunged the knife into Charles' stomach.

Chills ran down my spine and I burrowed under the yellow comforter. Hopefully, Ringo was faring well during our absence. Mrs. Wilson had always been nice to our cat, but she'd never watched him before. That had been Charles' job.

Ugh. Poor guy. His life hadn't been easy and I hoped he'd finally found peace in his death.

Those cops better bring him justice.

Chapter 19

As we arrived at the airport for our flight home, I felt pleasantly refreshed, even though I had slept only three hours. My only guess as to the reason why: I'd been able to forget about the stress of Charles' death for a few hours and enjoy myself. I hoped my energy would carry through the day, but if not, I'd have to rely on my coffee pot.

Donna, on the other hand, looked a little green. As we strode through the airport, she kept her sunglasses on and her gaze focused straight ahead while Marsha and I smiled and waved enough for the three of us.

At inspection, I was again assigned the front of the plane, and Donna rolled her eyes when she was told she'd be in back. Once we reached our aircraft, we said hello to the rest of the crew and began our pre-flight inspections. Donna poured herself a vodka and slammed it back, then washed out the glass. When our gazes met, her cheeks flushed pink, but I wasn't sure if it was because the alcohol had hit her system or she'd been embarrassed she'd been caught.

"Hair of the dog," she whispered.

I nodded and continued with preparation. Perhaps it was time for Donna to dry out, at least for a little while. I'd consider talking to her about it when we got home.

As the passengers embarked, I smiled and sized them up. A couple boarded with a toddler in tow. The mother's gaze met mine, her eyes almost lifeless with absolute exhaustion. As the child reached for his father's hand, the man pulled away from the boy, completely ignoring him. An absent father, no doubt—physically there, but unavailable. I followed them to their seat and bit my tongue as I took the man's coat while he insisted the child sit by the window and he take the aisle seat. Such a shame. I'd have to make sure the boy enjoyed the flight and maybe slip the mother a little extra alcohol in her cocktail if she asked for one.

I met the gaze of another man who sweated

profusely. Sweaty Sam. Smiling, he wiped his brow. "Sorry, I'm a bit nervous. They say air travel is safe but flying through the air in a tin can doesn't make me feel that way."

"It's fine, sir," I said, gently placing my hand on his shoulder. "We're here to make sure you have a wonderful, relaxing, and very safe flight. May I take your coat and fetch you something to ease your nerves?"

Two beers later, he slept soundly, and I prayed there wouldn't be any turbulence. People like him really got upset and afraid, making the flight difficult for the crew and everyone around him.

After takeoff, we prepared the lunch—seared salmon or baked chicken with rice and a salad. Once cleanup was over and all my customers seemed content, I hurried back to check on Donna.

"How's it going?" I asked, sidling up to her in the galley.

"Great!" she said, smiling while lining up glasses on a tray.

"You feeling okay?"

She nodded but didn't meet my stare. I glanced over my shoulder to make sure no one was listening. "Have you had more to drink?" I whispered.

"I'm fine," she hissed. "Go back to your customers."

With a sigh I shook my head. I could smell the alcohol.

"Donna, you can't drink while you're working."

"What am I supposed to do? The man in 20-A asked me to join him, so I did. No one noticed. It's fine."

I almost replied, but then I noted someone was in the bathroom. The last thing we needed was a passenger listening in on our conversation, but I was quite irritated with my friend.

If something were to happen with our plane, Donna's drinking was not only a safety hazard to the customers, but also to the crew. Everyone needed to be firing on all cylinders, so to speak. Any lingering doubt I'd had about speaking to her in regard to her drinking flew out the window. We'd be having a long chat when we landed and rested at home.

Just as I turned to walk up the aisle back to my own station, a voice called from the restroom. "Hello?"

I placed my ear against the door. "Yes, sir?"

"The... uh... the door won't open."

Donna and I exchanged glances.

"Sir, did you unlock the door?" I asked as Donna slid past me to deliver her drinks.

"Y-yes. It's jammed. I've been trying to get out of here for at least ten minutes. Please. Help me!"

While I pushed and pulled on the door, some of the customers in the back row offered to help. Donna asked they remain in their seats. Having a bunch of people up and about would lead to injuries if we ran into turbulence.

"Can you open it?" the man asked.

I thought I recognized the trembling voice but wanted to double-check I was correct. "I'll be right back."

"Don't leave me in here!"

"I'm going to find someone to help, sir. Just one moment. Try to relax."

As I hurried up to the front of the plane, I passed Sweaty Sam's empty seat and groaned. The one person who was already a nervous wreck was now trapped in the bathroom.

"What's going on?" Marsha whispered as I rushed into the galley.

"There's a man trapped in the back bathroom. He was scared to fly to begin with, and now he can't open the door.

Marsha closed her eyes and sighed. "I knew this

trip was going too smoothly. We better fetch one of the pilots and see if they can somehow finagle that thing open."

I knocked on the cockpit door and stuck my head in when summoned. The controls never failed to amaze me. How they kept track of what all the buttons, switches and dials did, I'd never understand.

"What's up, Patty?" Large Larry asked, turning to me.

"We have an issue in the back bathroom. One of the customers can't get the door open."

"Sounds like a job for you, Larry," the captain said with a chuckle. "If anyone's strong enough to break down that door, it's you."

"I'll have a look," he said, unbuckling his seat belt. He couldn't stand at his full height in the cockpit, so he remained hunched over.

He followed me down the aisle, saying hello to a few passengers. With his uniform and size, he cut an impressive figure. Once we reached the back, he smiled at Donna who was preparing another tray of drinks. If I remembered correctly, they'd had a fling in the past and it had ended on pleasant terms.

"Sir," Larry called. "My name's Larry Goodwin. I'm the co-pilot and I'm going to see what I can do to get you out of here."

"T-thank you."

Larry pushed and pulled on the door, just as I had, then shook his head. He motioned for me to follow him to the front.

"That door folds inward, toward the passenger," Larry said quietly as we huddled together in the galley. "I could break it, but I'm wondering if it's best just to keep him in there until maintenance can take it off and free him. If I push too hard, it could fly inward and hurt him.

The lavatory didn't offer any room for Sweaty Sam to move out of the way. A person could stand, or they could sit. Chances were good that if Larry broke the door, he may break Sweaty Sam's face as well.

Shaking my head, I pursed my lips together. "We can't take that risk. He's a nervous flier, which makes this all the worse."

Larry sighed and crossed his arms over his chest. "What do you think? Leave him in there and hope he doesn't have a heart attack, or let me break the door and hope we don't smash his nose?"

Marsha had been rushing in and out of the galley, working around us to serve the customers.

She set down her tray and joined us. "We're close to Utah, aren't we?"

Larry nodded.

"I think we should leave him and make an emergency landing. Patty, you stand next to the door and try to keep him calm. Donna and I can start cleanup a little early and finish it without you. Breaking in the door is only going to cause more commotion and stress for the rest of the passengers."

She had a valid point.

Pulling out the clipboard with a map of the plane, names of passengers and their assigned seating, she announced his name. "Samuel Jones."

Wow. I'd been spot on with the moniker I'd given him.

"I'll talk to the captain. I'm sure he'll want to land, then I'll radio into Salt Lake City and let them know the situation," Larry said.

As I returned to the back of the plane, I tried to think of ways to keep Sweaty Sam calm, and came up with a fat zero. How did one pacify a nervous flier stuck in a bathroom?

Unfortunately, I couldn't recall any previous training on the matter. Perhaps that should be rectified for new stews.

I whispered our plan to Donna, who nodded in agreement. "I think he's crying," she said. "He's very upset."

A grown man crying wasn't something I wanted to deal with, but I'd been tasked with it, so I would.

I knocked on the restroom door. "Mr. Jones?"

"Y-yes?"

"Sir, we're almost at Salt Lake, where we're going to land. At this time, we believe it's best for you to remain in there."

"No! No... you can't do that to me."

"If we try to break down the door, we're afraid it will hurt you. You don't want a broken nose, do you?" His silence indicated he was actually weighing his options. Unfortunately, he didn't have a choice in the matter. "I'm going to stay right here with you," I continued. "Why don't you tell me a little about yourself?"

"I'm stuck in a toilet in a tin can speeding through space."

Exactly what I didn't want him thinking about.

"Are you married?" I asked, crossing my arms over my chest and leaning my forehead against the door.

"Yes. Ten years."

"And what's her name?"

"Mildred."

"Kids?"

"Five."

"How old are they?"

As he listed his children's names and ages, Donna and Marsha hustled throughout the plane to clean up before landing. A few passengers glanced over their shoulders at me speaking to the lavatory door, but I only smiled and motioned for them to turn around. *Nothing to see here, folks.*

"You mentioned little Mary was a dancer," I said. "Does she do ballet or some other form?"

"Tap. She's a tap dancer," Sweaty Sam replied. He grew quiet for a long moment, then began sobbing again. "I may never watch her dance again."

"Don't you think like that," I scolded. "Everything is going to be just fine."

The plane dropped and I braced myself in between the two walls.

"We're going to crash," Sam muttered. "I'm going to die in a toilet."

"It's just a little turbulence," I spoke soothingly. "We get it often flying into Utah. It's nothing to worry about."

A few passengers squealed at the next bump.

The third one caused me to lose my balance and I almost toppled over to the floor.

"The captain has advised that everyone take their seats," Marsha said over the intercom. "Please make sure your seatbelt is buckled. We will be making an emergency stop in Utah."

Some passengers groaned in irritation.

"That means you too, Patty," Donna said. "You better grab a seat."

"What about him?" I asked, hitching my thumb over my shoulder. "I can't leave him."

"You're going to have to. Being up and around is a hazard, not only to yourself, but to everyone around you."

Pretty rich coming from the drunk stew, but I wouldn't argue. I turned back to the restroom. I couldn't remember Sweaty Sam's last name. "Sir? I need to sit down now. I advise you to do the same."

As the plane jumped again, I made my way over to the jump seat Donna had pulled out for me, steadying myself on the walls.

When I reached it, I quickly snapped the belt and shut my eyes. I had full faith in our captains to land us safely but turbulence was the one thing I really hated about flying because I became ill with motion sickness so easily. My stomach rolled with the plane. Thankfully, I hadn't had anything to eat. If I had, I may have lost it all over the galley.

From the lavatory, I thought I heard prayers being whispered.

I didn't blame him. The plane leapt around like a wayward soccer ball. I'd been on plenty of rough flights, but the aircraft seemed out of control as it bounced. Despite my confidence in the captains, I considered that we may die.

It never hurt to pray so I sent up a silent request that our lives be spared. I didn't want to die in an airplane crash.

Chapter 20

ONCE OUR WHEELS TOUCHED DOWN AND WE CAME to a halt, it seemed like everyone gave one collective sigh of relief. Donna and I traded weary smiles. We hadn't died.

"That was a rough landing," she said. "I actually feel a little queasy."

"Me, too. "I better check on our bathroom guest."

I unbuckled my seatbelt and stood, as did Donna. While she fetched coats and helped people retrieve their bags from the overhead bins, I tried to stay out of the way. Unfortunately, with the bathroom door being out of order, everyone would have to debark and the airline would find us another plane to take to San Francisco. It was going to be a long afternoon, and if we didn't arrive back home until late night, it would be no surprise.

"Sir?" I tapped on the door.

No answer. I couldn't recall his last name. *Forget formalities.*

"Sam?"

Again, I was met with silence.

What if he'd died from an anxiety induced heart attack?

As the passengers filed out the front, two members of the maintenance crew came in through the back.

"There's something wrong with him," I said. "Hurry! We need to get in there!"

We should have tried to break him out. Never had I experienced such horrible turbulence, and I couldn't imagine trying to ride it out in the lavatory.

As they worked on the panel, I reviewed cardiopulmonary resuscitation instructions from memory just in case I needed to perform them once the door came off.

"How are things going back here?" Marsha asked once all the passengers had deplaned. "We sure have a lot of angry customers over this."

"Over a man being trapped in the lavatory?" I

asked. "Why are they upset? They aren't the ones in there!"

"They wanted us to continue to San Francisco. No regard for anyone but themselves and their own schedules."

"He's not responding to me," I said, trying to remain calm and professional, not caring the least bit that people were upset their trip had been interrupted. "I think we better call in medical."

She nodded and hurried back down the aisle just as the maintenance crew removed the door to reveal Sweaty Sam sitting on the closed toilet, completely passed out, his face as white as the rice I'd served earlier. We all stared at him a moment, and I figured everyone was as taken aback as I was.

"Is he dead?" Donna asked when Marsha returned. "He looks dead." I didn't argue. She wasn't wrong.

Marsha moved in and placed her hand in front of his mouth. "He's breathing."

"Check his pulse," Donna said.

My heart thundered as Marsha's hand moved to Sam's neck. Maybe I was the one who was going into cardiac arrest?

"His skin is clammy, but we have a pulse," Marsha announced. At last, the two pilots rushed down the aisle toward us. We all sighed in relief. "Medical will be here in a minute," Marsha continued, her voice calm and reassuring, which was why she was the head stew. "For now, I say we leave him right where he is until they get here. We don't know how badly he got knocked around in there during the turbulence."

The captains nodded in agreement.

A short period later, medical personnel arrived and maneuvered Sam out of the restroom and onto a stretcher. We gathered our things and followed them off. A man with a clipboard waited at the bottom of the stairs wearing a suit—obviously airline management. Going from cigarette smoke to the smell of airplane fuel made me cough, and I longed for some fresh air.

"This whole crew will be moving to Gate 3C and using the plane there to finish the flight to San Fran," he said, his voice clipped. "Are we clear?"

The five of us nodded.

"Good. Run along now. We're steering the passengers over that way as I speak. They need their crew to get the plane in the air."

Thankfully, the flight from Utah to San Francisco went off without anyone being trapped in the lavatory, no overly drunk people, and only one screaming child. When I stepped off the plane, exhaustion roiled through me and I couldn't wait to get home.

"Would you ladies like to grab a drink with us?" Large Larry asked. "I think we all deserve one after that New York flight."

"Has anyone heard if Sam's okay?" I asked. Going for cocktails was the last thing on my mind. I worried that our decision to leave him in the restroom had killed the poor man.

"No word at all, but hopefully they'll let us know," Marsha said. "And I for one would love a glass of wine."

"Count me in, too," Donna said.

I shook my head. "Not for me. I'm heading home."

"Don't be such a downer, Patty," Donna said. "Come join us!"

"No, thank you. I'll see you all sometime soon!"

I didn't wait to be chided further. Instead, I grabbed my bag and hurried through the airport while dreaming of slipping off my girdle and curling up on the couch with Ringo. A blast of cool, damp air hit me as I exited the airport. I inhaled deeply, glancing up at the sky. Sprinkles of raindrops pelted my face and a chill ran down my spine as the cold took its grip. Finally, fresh air.

As I slid into the cab, I did wish Donna would have come home with me. The thought of going into our empty apartment alone gave me a case of the jitters. Would I find a murderer waiting for me? Or a cat that had peed on everything? And which would be worse?

How Donna kept up with her lifestyle, I'd never understand.

When the cab pulled in front of the apartment building, I paid and then exited. Our super, Mr. Killian, was planting flowers in the new planters installed outside the building. The pink and purple petunias really added a nice touch to the front entrance.

"They look wonderful, Mr. Killian!"

He rose to standing and grinned. "I think so, too. I only hope no one comes along and picks them. I'd hate to have all this work destroyed."

"I'm sure they'll be fine," I said. "People still respect others' property."

He placed his hands on his hips. "Tell that to those dang protestors. Where are you coming back from?"

"We started this morning in New York, then to Utah and here."

"Busy day."

I laughed and shook my head. "You have no idea, Mr. Killian. I can't wait to get out of this uniform and relax for a bit."

"Well, don't let me stop you. Have a nice evening, little lady."

Instead of trudging up the stairs, I waited patiently for the elevator. When the doors parted, I stepped inside, pressed the button to my floor, and leaned against the wall. The short ride seemed to take forever.

I pulled out the keys to my apartment as I exited the elevator. Just as I pushed open my door, Mrs. Wilson came out into the hallway carrying Ringo.

"Patty!" she exclaimed with a wide grin. "I was just going to fetch some food for this sweet prince."

"Thank you so much," I said as she handed the tabby off to me. "We felt awful about dropping him in your lap like that, but the call came in before dawn that we had to work. We had no notice and he doesn't like being alone."

"It was no trouble at all, dear. I was happy to help you out." Ringo jumped from my arms and into the apartment, scurrying across the living room and into the bedroom. "So tell me about your travels."

"Come on in," I said, motioning for her to follow me. "Have I got a story for you!" I dropped my bags by the door. "Take a seat. I'm just going to change really quick. I'll be right back."

I found Ringo sitting on top of a bed pillow, glaring at me, when I entered the bedroom. "I'm sorry we had to leave," I whispered as I undressed. "We need to work to buy you food. How was your time with Mrs. Wilson?"

He shut his eyes and turned away from me.

Ugh. Such a cranky cat.

Once I'd slipped on a pair of sweatpants and a T-shirt, I joined Mrs. Wilson in the living room.

"I hope you don't mind, Patty. I helped myself to some tea."

"Not at all," I replied, sinking into the couch. "You're always welcome here."

"Thank you, dear. Now tell me your tale! You've got my mind spinning with what it may be!"

As I told her the story of the passenger trapped in the bathroom, I tried to remember every detail. My memory for names might not be the best, but since meeting Bill Hart, I was focusing on remembering things I'd normally overlook—like the color of Sam's shirt and the time of day when he'd first reached out for help.

Once I finished my story, Mrs. Wilson stared at me wide-eyed, enthralled by my tale, her tea disregarded.

"My word," she muttered, shaking her head. "I'm not sure whether to laugh or cry for that poor man."

I nodded in agreement. "Hopefully, we'll find out he's just fine. It was a terrible thing to happen to anyone, but he was nervous before he even stepped foot on the tarmac."

"What a shame. I hope they put some mechanical thing in place to prevent that from happening again." Smart woman. After the incident, it seemed they'd do something to avoid future passenger trappings.

"Have you heard any more about Charles' murder?" I asked. "Has the police been by?"

"No. It's been so quiet. I hate to say it, but with Charles gone, I'm sleeping through the night and not waking up to his screaming any longer, bless his soul."

"How odd," I replied. "I would think the police would have come to talk to us again."

"I'm afraid not. I worry that they are just going

to let the murder slide and it'll become another cold case. There's so much crime these days, I wouldn't be the least bit surprised if that's what happened."

"It would be a shame," I said, completely uncomfortable with the idea. "That would mean that a murderer could possibly be living in our building! Or walking the streets ready to strike again!"

"Oh, I'm aware of that. It's truly frightening, especially for women like us who live alone. At times like these, I wish my husband was still alive."

And I wished Donna had come home with me.

"I better get going, Patty. I'll leave you to rest."

Standing, I walked her to the door, then bent down and gave her a hug. "Thanks again, Mrs. Wilson. I appreciate you so much."

"The feeling is mutual, Patty. I couldn't ask for better neighbors."

Just as I was about to shut the door, she turned to me. "Oh! I should give you your key back." She fished it from her pocket and placed it in my palm. "Here you go. Anytime you need me to watch Ringo, just let me know."

I shut the door behind me, walked over to the key drawer and tossed it in. After it landed with a clink, I gazed at it for a moment before picking it up again.

As I held it up in front of my face, my heart raced and sweat broke out on my brow. "I think I'm going to pass out."

Gripping the counter with one hand, I grabbed the other two keychains from the drawer and brought them all over to the couch, then flipped on the side table lamp. Laying all the keys out on the coffee table, I stared at them for a long time.

My goodness.

Had I just discovered the murderer?

Chapter 21

I GRABBED A PAD OF PAPER AND PEN FROM THE SIDE table and wrote with a shaky hand.

Motive.

Opportunity.

Once I filled those out and jotted other miscellaneous notes and a timeline, I tossed the notebook to the side and rubbed my temples. I had either solved a murder or I was losing my mind.

A knock sounded at the door, but I didn't answer. Too distracted. Besides, what if it was the killer?

I hesitated to share my findings. After all, I'd been reminded many times I wasn't a police officer and had no training in the art of finding killers. But yet, as I stared at my notebook and the keys, I realized I had to tell someone. And if I was wrong? I'd be the stupid stew with an overactive imagination. If I was right... well, I'd just solved a murder.

Which was more important? Justice for Charles or my delicate ego? I'd been underestimated my entire life, so I was used to that. But Charles deserved to have his killer put away. Those surrounding the case deserved safety.

After locating Detective Peterson's number, I picked up the phone and dialed, my hands still trembling. My call was answered on the second ring when I was told Detective Peterson wasn't in and I'd need to leave a message.

"Please tell him Patricia Byrne called regarding the Charles Bernard murder."

When I hung up, I immediately decided to phone Bill. If he could use his badge and crankiness to track down a stew in New York, he could hunt down a cop in San Francisco. I hurried to my bag and fetched his number then returned to the couch. After dialing, I studied the evidence in front of me. All of it was well and good, but I had no proof. Only a very strong suspicion.

"Bill Hart," he answered with a sigh, as if his phone had rung far too many times during the day.

"Bill, it's Patty Byrne."

"Well, hello, Patty. It's nice to hear your voice."

"I think I may have solved Charles' murder."

A moment of heavy silence fell, then he burst out laughing. I listened to him chuckle for a good thirty seconds as I twisted the phone cord around my finger, growing more irritated by the moment.

"Okay, Patty. Now I'm curious. Tell me how *you've* solved a murder that the police haven't."

And there was the rub. Who did I think I was, calling the FBI with my crazy conjecture? "I didn't say I solved it," I muttered. "I said I *may* have solved it."

"I'm all ears. Tell me your theory."

"I think Mrs. Wilson killed Charles."

He hesitated a beat before asking, "The little old lady?"

"Yes."

"Patty, have you been downstairs smoking dope with the hippies?"

"No! Just listen to me!"

"Do you have any proof? Like did she confess or show you the bloody knife?"

"No."

"She's a sweet, old woman, Patty. I don't see how—"

"Will you please stop talking and listen?!"

"Fine," he replied with a huff. "This should be rich."

A knock sounded at my door again, but I ignored it and took a deep breath while keeping my gaze focused on the paper in front of me. Ringo pranced out of the bedroom and curled up on the couch next to me, as if urging me on, yet comforting me at the same time. "I just got back from New York and we had left a key for Mrs. Wilson to use to come in and feed Ringo."

"Okay..."

"Well, when she gave it back to me a little while ago, I realized that Donna had left her the wrong key. She'd given Mrs. Wilson the key to Charles' apartment, the one he'd given us."

"And?"

"There was no way for her to access our apartment while we were gone, Bill. We'd never exchanged keys with her, but we had with Charles."

"I'm confused, Patty."

Closing my eyes, I rubbed my temple again with one hand while holding the phone with the other. The headache seemed to be growing worse by the second. "Charles had our key. Mrs. Wilson didn't, but she *did* have a key to Charles' apartment. I've seen her use it. What if after Charles died, she went in and made copies of our key and used it to feed Ringo?"

"What if she grabbed your key from Charles' apartment to take care of the cat?"

I shook my head. "We took it back a couple of days ago. She had to have made a copy before then."

Bill remained silent for a long while. "Even if she did make a copy of your key from Charles' apartment, that doesn't make her a murderer. What's her motive?"

"Charles' nightmares. She's mentioned how much they scared her and how they kept her awake. She said since his death she's sleeping so much better. She hated the screaming."

It sounded as if Bill was tapping a pen against the table. "A sixty-something-year-old lady doesn't kill out of the blue."

"What if she's done it before and gotten away with it?"

"What are you talking about?"

"Her husband," I said with a sigh. "He died falling down the stairs here in the apartment building a few years ago. What if it wasn't an accident? What if she pushed him? Or tripped him?"

"I think you're grasping at straws," Bill replied.

"What happened to your suspicions about the girl-friend, Karen? Or the wife, Claudia?"

"I've thought about that. Here's the thing: Mrs. Wilson has been there every step of the way, casting doubt away from herself and onto everyone else, planting seeds and ideas in everyone's head. I didn't even realize she was doing that until just a few moments ago. She called Claudia a shrew, but then was rude and mean to her to force her to act like a harpy. We found a will that Charles had supposedly typed mixed in with a book he'd been writing that stated Karen was to get his estate. Mrs. Wilson had access to the apartment so she could have typed that out and slipped it in the stack of papers for someone to find, which would have been Karen's motive. She also said Wayne, Charles' friend, is a drug dealer, which is true, so he's seedy and could've killed Charles."

"What about the hippy downstairs?"

In-the-Buff Bob. "She told me she hated the way he treated Charles and he could've done it as well. Don't you see? She's actively worked to cast blame anywhere but on herself."

"Let me think about this," Bill grumbled.

I remained quiet, tossing around all the pieces of the puzzle. "One other thing," I said. "We found a note under our pillow that was a threat, telling us not to get too close or we'd be next. It had been typed on Charles' typewriter."

"How do you know that?"

"I went over there and looked at the ribbon. I could make out the words on it."

"And Mrs. Wilson had access to Charles' apartment?"

"Yes. They'd traded keys."

"Wouldn't you have heard her stabbing him? I'm assuming he would have yelled for help or something."

"Not necessarily. Donna and I weren't here, but even if Mrs. Wilson killed Charles after I got home, I probably wouldn't have heard anything. The anti-war protesters were so loud, I couldn't have the window open. I also had music on while I tidied up."

"Interesting." He was finally taking me seriously!

"She knew him, Bill. She could have walked right up to him and shoved that knife into him. He never would have felt threatened by her, because as you said, she's a sweet, little old lady. They were friends and neighbors."

"And you think she has the physical strength to do something like that?"

"She may be older, but she's not infirm. Mrs. Wilson is a strong woman."

"You put all this together over a key?" Bill asked, his voice incredulous.

"When she handed it back to me, I realized Donna had left her the wrong one. In order for her to get Ringo, that meant she'd have to have made a copy of ours, which she'd retrieved from Charles' apartment. No one else has a key."

"Karen had access to Charles' apartment. I'm assuming she had a key since she was the girlfriend. And what about Claudia? You said you found her inside the apartment looking for a will. They both had access."

Yes, the one little detail that put a dent in my theory. "I know. But I think someone needs to take a look at Mrs. Wilson, Bill. She had motive and opportunity, and she's placed herself in the middle of the investigation but has cast suspicion on everyone else."

"What if Claudia killed him for money?"

"If I were Claudia, I'd make sure I had that will in hand before murdering him. When Mrs. Wilson and I found her in Charles' apartment, she freely admitted she was searching for it. She didn't have it. Why kill him over money when she can't prove she's the beneficiary?"

"And Karen?"

"She had recently found out that he was married, but she's not a killer. She's too... fragile, almost broken."

"And Wayne? He was at the apartment twice that day."

"No. He lost a friend. He didn't care about the money Charles owed him."

"The hippy?"

I sighed and ran a hand through my hair. "Honestly, I don't see it. He's too high and into his peace and love to kill. At least I think so. I think he likes spouting his views, but I don't see him having the wherewithal to murder anyone."

It wasn't worth mentioning that Ringo had also scampered away from Mrs. Wilson when I arrived home and met her in the hallway just over an hour ago. The cat's reaction wouldn't be an important part of evidence to a police officer, but to me, it showed a lot. Ringo had been there when Charles was killed and he'd run from Mrs. Wilson, probably only spending time with her so he'd be fed and not alone.

Bill tapped his pen loudly. "Okay, I'm going to call Peterson and have him come over there. Are you going to be home for a while?"

"Yes."

"He'll probably want to see you either tonight or first thing in the morning. I'll have him call you immediately."

"Thanks, Bill."

"And Patty?"

"Hmm?"

"If you're right about this and he can nail Mrs. Wilson, you've done some fine police work."

A slow blush crawled up my neck and into my cheeks. Accolades from the FBI agent? I'd take it. "Thanks."

"I'll talk to you soon."

After I slowly set the phone back on the cradle, I sat back against the cushions and closed my eyes. If I dug through enough drawers, I'd hopefully find the cigarette I craved so badly. But did I have the energy to even rise from the couch?

Yes. I also needed a glass of water. Ringo meowed loudly, then scampered away, obviously upset about something.

When I opened my eyes and stood, I found Mrs. Wilson leaning against the front door.

Chapter 22

HOW IN THE HECK... HAD I LEFT THE DOOR unlocked, or had she used the key I suspected she had in her possession? I really needed to pay more attention to that.

"Hello, Patty," she said sweetly, standing with her hands clasped behind her back.

I studied every detail of her. She wore a light blue pair of slacks, a white sweater and blue flats. Her normally friendly smile had disappeared and she stared at me with hard, cold blue eyes that sent a shiver down my spine.

"M-Mrs. Wilson!" I said, my voice a little high, despite my attempts to act as if I weren't scared to death. "I didn't hear you come in!"

"I was knocking, but there wasn't an answer."

Stepping back and to my left, I placed the coffee table in between us. "I'm sorry about that. I-I was on the phone." Glancing down at the table, I noted the keys. Hopefully, she didn't notice.

"I was going to leave you be until I heard my name."

Dang it! "Are you sure you did? I wasn't speaking about you. I don't like to gossip. That would be rude."

Of course, I was lying. Donna and I gossiped with her all the time.

"Oh, I'm very sure I heard my name," Mrs. Wilson said, walking toward me. "Please tell me who you were talking to."

"Just a friend, Mrs. Wilson."

"Do you always speculate on murder with your friends like that?"

I swallowed past the lump in my throat. What was she hiding behind her back? Could she be ready to kill me as well?

"I knew my plan was risky," Mrs. Wilson said. "But I couldn't take it anymore. Charles screaming at all hours of the night, the fights with Claudia... all I want is to live the last years of my life in peace, and that man made it impossible."

Oh, my word. I'd been right! Yet, she kept

approaching me, her hands still behind her back. I was literally trapped, the coffee table to my front, the wall to my back, the couch to my left. The only place I could go was the bedroom, and it seemed that would only corner me further.

Perhaps I should keep her talking? "W-why didn't you just move?" I asked.

"*I* was here first. I *like* living here. This is *my* neighborhood. Everyone and everything I know is here. I shouldn't have to go anywhere to find a peaceful life."

"But killing someone… that seems so extreme."

"I learned long ago to get rid of the people in my life who bring me unhappiness."

Both fascinated and horrified, I listened intently while keeping her talking and trying to figure a way out of my apartment and to safety.

"Is that what happened with your husband?" I asked. "Did he make you unhappy?"

"He was a typical man, expecting me to wait on him. I tired of being his maid, bless his soul."

"So you pushed him down the stairs?"

Mrs. Wilson shrugged and her mouth turned up in a slight grin. "I crushed a few sleeping pills in the mashed potatoes and led him out to the landing. He barely needed my help down the stairs."

The coffee table was the only thing that separated us now.

"I really put a wrench in my plan by handing you the key today," Mrs. Wilson continued. "I never thought a stupid stewardess would have noticed. I thought it would be easy to come in here and exchange it with the correct one. I knew where you girls keep them, because as you guessed, I've been in here before."

"You left the note?"

"Yes. With you hanging out with your FBI agent, you got me worried. I thought I'd throw in a little assurance to keep your nose out of the investigation. I wasn't worried about the police—they'd never suspect the little old lady to kill a man."

"You're quite sneaky," I said. "You manipulated everyone close to Charles. You made everyone look guilty... but you."

"I did," Mrs. Wilson said. "I thought they'd pin it on Wayne or Claudia for sure. Those two had the most to gain, but I also needed to throw Karen into the mix. She's weak and an easy target. I typed up that will, hoping the police would find it."

"They didn't. But my friends and I did."

"Yes," she replied with a sigh. "The police weren't too bright either, were they?"

I shook my head as she came around the side of the coffee table, pinning me against the wall and the couch. She pulled her hand from behind her back to reveal a knife.

"You got in over your head, Patty. I'm sorry I have to do this. I do like you and Donna, despite her being a drunk harlot. I'll miss our chats."

"The cops are on their way!" I blurted. "They'll be here any minute! They know everything!"

"No, they don't. They know conjecture from a stupid stew. They have no proof. When they arrive, I'll be the grieving widow scared out of my mind that another one of my neighbors has been killed. Who do you think they're going to believe? The sweet old lady, or the young, dumb stewardess?"

That was the second—or maybe third?— time she'd called me dumb, and frankly I was tired of it. I'd proved just how smart I was… I'd solved a murder.

Yet, as she drew closer, I debated what to use as a weapon. There was no way for me to move fast enough between the couch and the coffee table. I'd fall for sure and give her an easy target to slam the knife. Hit her over the head with the lamp? I'd have to unplug it.

But then an idea came to me. Before I could

fully think it through, I grabbed the crutch leaning in the corner and, with a scream, raised it over my head and slammed it over hers. That bought me enough time to race for the front door as she dropped the knife and slowly sank to the floor.

When I opened the door, I ran into the chest of Detective Peterson.

"Patty?" he said, grabbing my shoulders.

The fear I'd experienced oozed out of me in sobs. My knees weakened as I pointed over my shoulder. "M-Mrs. Wilson," I stuttered. "She just confessed everything to me. S-she tried to kill me. With a knife."

Detective Peterson's eyes widened as he propped me up against the wall. "Stay out here."

I sank to the floor and held my head in my trembling hands as the tears kept coming. After a moment, I glanced around the corner into my apartment. Detective Peterson was helping Mrs. Wilson to her feet. She wobbled as she grabbed her head, the knife still visible on the floor.

"What is going on?" she asked. "Do you see what that girl did to me?"

"You're under arrest, ma'am," Peterson said.

"For what? For being beaten with a crutch?"

"For murder."

Mrs. Wilson turned a shade of red I'd never seen before and began to scream. I placed my hands over my ears, the sound resembling something I imagined Satan emitting—high pitched, guttural, and straight from a black, decrepit soul.

As he walked her out, the neighbors who lived on the other side me, Rainbow and Dusk, opened their door.

"What's going on, Patty?" Rainbow asked, crouching down next to me. Thankfully, she was clothed. Her bright, beautiful face pinched with worry, and next to Mrs. Wilson, she reminded me of an angel from heaven.

"Mrs. Wilson killed Charles," I whispered as I wiped my cheeks. "Then she tried to kill me."

"Oh, my. Is Donna home?"

I shook my head.

"Come inside with me," Rainbow said. "I'll fix you some tea to calm your nerves."

After allowing her to help me stand, I followed her inside the apartment, relieved that the murder was finally solved.

And I'd done it. Alone.

The stupid stew had solved the murder.

Look out, FBI. I'm coming.

Epilogue

DONNA ARRIVED HOME LATER THAT NIGHT. Frankly, I was surprised when I discovered she was mostly sober. I sipped on my third cup of tea, waiting for the brew Rainbow had provided to calm my nerves. I hadn't asked what was in it, but she assured me it would work. I just didn't know how much more I could drink.

"What's going on here?" she asked, flopping down on the sofa next to me. "I'm so exhausted and my feet are killing me. I hope they allow us to wear flat shoes the next time they update the uniforms."

"Mrs. Wilson killed Charles."

With a gasp, she sat up and turned toward me. "Are you serious?"

"Yes. I figured it out and she came after me with a knife. She admitted it all."

"Oh, my goodness," she whispered, bringing her hand to her mouth. "Are you okay?"

I had to consider the question for a moment. Having my life threatened and finding out I'd shared tea and wine with a killer had rattled me emotionally, but physically, I was fine. "Yes," I finally answered.

"Tell me everything."

As I recounted the whole ordeal, Donna stared at me wide-eyed.

"Unbelievable," she whispered, shaking her head. "I never would have guessed Mrs. Wilson in a hundred years."

"I know. But we have other things to talk about, Donna."

"We do?"

"Yes. I wanted to discuss your drinking."

She rolled her eyes and sat back on the couch. "I don't."

The phone rang, and I muttered a curse as I stood to answer it. "Hello?"

"Is this Patty or Donna?"

"This is Patty. Who is speaking, please?"

"It's Linda Davenport, Patty."

I glanced over my shoulder at Donna who had laid her head back against the cushions and closed her eyes. Neither of us had enough energy to jump back on a plane, and I wished I'd never answered. "What can I do for you, Linda?"

"Well, I wanted to let you know that customer that was trapped in the lavatory… what was his name… Samuel Jones. He's resting comfortably in the hospital and he'll be released tomorrow."

"Oh, thank goodness," I said, sighing. "I'm so glad to hear it."

Despite my run-in with Mrs. Wilson, I had been wondering about Sweaty Sam.

"Yes. We all were. Have a lovely night, dear."

I hung up the phone and relayed the news to Donna. "That's good," she replied with a yawn as she stretched her arms over her head. "Do you mind if I take the bed tonight?"

"Well, I'd really like to talk to you about—"

"Patty, I don't want to hear it, okay? I know I shouldn't have been drinking on the plane. Spare me the lecture."

I bit my lip and stared at her for a long moment, then motioned toward the bedroom. "Go ahead and take it. Maybe we can discuss things tomorrow."

Donna snorted and shook her head, then waltzed into the bedroom, leaving me alone with my thoughts. With a groan, I stretched out onto the couch. A moment later, Ringo jumped up and sat on my stomach. Shutting my eyes, I caressed his head.

The killer had been caught. *By me.*

For the time being, I'd been promoted to the front of the plane.

I'd met an FBI agent who interested me, but I wasn't quite sure if it was because of his career, or his dreamy green eyes.

Things were going pretty well, and I expected my life to return normal.

Certainly, there couldn't be any more murders to solve… right?

Will Donna straighten herself out, or will it only lead to more trouble? And what about Bill and Patty? Does he really have feelings for her?

To be notified of the next book in the Killer Skies Mysteries, In Plane Sight, please go here.

Also by Carly Winter

The Tri-Town Murders

Complete Series

Follow newspaper reporter Tilly and her group of fun,
quirky friends as they solve murders in a fictional, small
town in California.

News and Nectarines (free at all ebook outlets)

News and Nachos

News and Nutmeg

News and Noodles

Sedona Spirits

As the owner of Sedona Bed and Breakfast, Bernadette
Maxwell has always played up the rumors that her
business was haunted. She's never believed it herself,
even though she can't explain the odd odors that
sometimes permeate the room or why a blast of cold air
comes out of nowhere... until she has an accident and
can suddenly see her resident ghost—her crazy, fun-
loving, hippie grandmother, Ruby.

Killer Skies Mysteries

Set in 1965, join Patty Byrne, stewardess extraordinaire, as she flies the skies and solves murders with the help of her friends... and one cute FBI agent!

About the Author

Carly Winter is the pen name for a USA Today best-selling and award-winning romance author.

When not writing, she enjoys spending time with her family, reading and enjoying the fantastic Arizona weather (except summer - she doesn't like summer). She does like dogs, wine and chocolate and wishes Christmas happened twice a year.

To be notified of new releases, book recommendations, to learn more about Carly and for your chance to win giveaways, subscribe to her newsletter.

For more information on her books, please visit:
CarlyWinterCozyMysteries.com

For release information only, not a newsletter, follow her on:
BookBub
Books2Read